BEAUTY LOOKS DOWN ON ME

STORIES

TRANSLATED BY YOONJIN PARK AND CRAIG BOTT, WITH ADDITIONAL TRANSLATION BY SORA KIM-RUSSELL AND JAE WON CHUNG

DALKEY ARCHIVE PRESS

Originally published in Korean as *Areumdaumi Nareul Myeolshihanda* by
Changbi Publishers in 2007.

Library of Congress Cataloging-in-Publication Data

Names: Un, Hui-gyong, 1959- author. | Yoonjin, Park, translator.
Title: Beauty looks down on me : stories / by Eun Heekyung.
Description: First Dalkey Archive edition. | Victoria, TX : Dalkey Archive Press,
2016.
Identifiers: LCCN 2016039382 | ISBN 9781628971774 (pbk. : alk. paper)
Classification: LCC PL992.845.H84 A2 2016 | DDC 895.73/4--dc23
LC record available at https://lccn.loc.gov/2016039382

Published in collaboration with the Literature Translation Institute of Korea.

The author would like to thank Alexis Diaz and Seanam Kim for their
assistance in her review of the translation.

www.dalkeyarchive.com
Victoria, TX / McLean, IL / Dublin

Dalkey Archive Press publications are, in part, made possible through the
support of the University of Houston-Victoria and its programs in creative
writing, publishing, and translation.

Printed on permanent/durable acid-free paper

BEAUTY LOOKS DOWN ON ME

Table of Contents

BEAUTY LOOKS DOWN ON ME

Spring Snow

I'LL NEVER FORGET the first time I saw Botticelli's *The Birth of Venus*. A late spring snow was coming down. As I followed my father into the carpeted Italian restaurant, I realized it was unlike any other place I'd ever known. Each table was set with its own dainty flower vase and candle sticks, and the air in the room was quietly stirred by the subdued conversations of affluent, refined-looking people skillfully handling Western-style silverware. My father and I were shown to a reserved table by a window. A waiter took my father's elegant overcoat and my old, lumpy parka and hung them on a coat stand.

As soon as I sat down across from him, my eyes went to a large painting dimly lit by a spotlight on the wall behind him. I couldn't look directly at him. The restaurant was warm and sweat soon began to pool along the folds of my neck. "Now that you're in middle school," he said, "you have to start taking care of your mother." I gave him the barest nod in response. "Feel free to call me anytime," he added. It sounded like a lie. When the food came out, I lowered my eyes and pretended to be busy eating. He dipped a shrimp in sauce and placed it on my plate. "You have a healthy appetite," he said. "But don't worry. The fat will melt off on its own when you grow up. When I was your age, everyone called me Tubby." That sounded like a lie too.

Once we'd finished eating and the plates were cleared away, I had nothing to distract me, so I gazed up at the painting again. He turned to see what I was looking at. The corners of his mouth

3

rose into a dignified smile. "Ah, Venus," he said. "Being born from the sea foam." Why did those words make me so sad? Was it her face, as smooth and beautiful as a porcelain doll's, milky-hued with just a hint of green? Or the long, blond hair whipping in the wind and wrapping around her slender, naked body? Or those bare white feet, so vulnerable, poised on a great gaping shell? Maybe it was the mysterious sorrow lurking deep in her eyes as she gazed down into space. "I'm sorry," my father said sadly, when he saw that my eyes were brimming with tears.

Looking back now, I realize that, as I followed my father around that day, I was tormented by the question of why I was born. Each time I fell behind, he had to stop and wait for me to catch up, probably thinking all the while, just as everyone else did, that I was slow because I was fat. I was already used to that kind of misunderstanding. Because I was fat, people always thought I looked unhappy or grumpy, when really I was just shy. Each time I saw my father, I went home feeling sad afterward because I was convinced I could never please him. I think he hated the fact that I was fat. If I'd been one of those clever, innocent kids, he'd have been the tragic hero, but a fat kid who looks stupid and grumpy all the time could never amount to anything more than a reminder of his past mistake, his one moment of folly.

Venus

WHEN I GOT old enough to buy things with my own money, I put a poster of Botticelli's Venus on my wall. Since it had a naked woman in it, my high school friends figured it meant I had a different taste in porn. B said fat people were obsessed with the classics as a form of psychological compensation, a way to prove how refined and sensitive we really were. But what interested me was not the sensuous Venus welcoming her lover Mars into bed, nor the pure, innocent Venus holding Eros as he drew back his bow. Even the Venus de Milo with her elegant, almost ideal symmetry, looked like a mere model for an art class to me. The only Venus in my book was Botticelli's.

That day, my friends and I went to B's house to sneak drinks of some whiskey his parents had brought back from a trip to Europe. Throughout the house were bottles of ginseng wine and other kinds of liquor that we were always stealing swigs from and topping the bottles off with water afterwards so his parents wouldn't know. But that day, we didn't dare drink too much, as B warned us over and over that it was expensive stuff. We decided to have just a tiny bit more of the whiskey that B's father kept in his study, and I went to get the bottle. I liked his father's study—the dust-covered books, the secrecy and solitude, the faint, manly scent hanging in the air. Of all the things B had, it was perhaps what I liked the most. I took the bottle from the bookcase, and, on my way out, stole a glance at the book lying open on the desk. I was always curious to know what B's father was reading. This one was a museum catalogue that looked like it had come from his latest trip.

5

On the page was a statuette of an immensely obese woman. A sagging roll of flesh around her middle made it look like she was carrying a baby on her back, wrapped tightly around with a thick cotton quilt. Her upper body learned forward to support breasts the size of stone mortars against a belly as round as a clay jar and short legs as thick as pillars. There was nothing that suggested arms, legs, neck, or waist, and her face as well had nothing that might be termed features. It looked like someone had stuck a pair of elephant's legs on a hastily rolled snowman. The woman's name was *The Venus of Willendorf*. The caption said it was a stone Venus made about 20,000 years ago during the Ice Age and was preserved in a museum in Vienna, Austria.

I couldn't take my eyes off of her; I felt possessed. I set the bottle down and carefully tore the page out of the catalogue. I folded it a couple of times and tucked it into my back pocket. Even now, I don't quite know why I stole the picture. Maybe it was my first vague sense of just how long ago twenty thousand years was. I could be a cliché and say that I felt a primal stirring somewhere deep inside, but the truth is that I was a lot more cynical about it at the time. But those feelings were immediately forgotten when my friends loudly welcomed me back into the room, bottle in hand. I forgot all about the stolen picture until I got home and took off my pants. Feeling drowsy from the alcohol, I carelessly slipped the picture between the pages of the first book I grabbed from the bookshelf and went straight to bed. As I threw myself onto it, the bed groaned as if being tortured.

I was probably at my heaviest around then. I still dream about the agony of high school gym classes sometimes. I all but forgot about the woman whose picture made me a thief for the first time in my life. But whenever I stood on the scale in the public bath on Sunday mornings when no one else was around, she'd come back to me. Each time, I'd get down from the scale, muttering, "Please, Venus, enough with the blessings. I don't need any more of your bounty or your fecundity." But I didn't think about her so often as to want to ransack all the books in my bookcase looking for that photo. I don't know why, but after I went to college, I bound my books together, in the same order as they'd been shelved, and sold them all to a secondhand bookstore. The faded picture of Botticelli's Venus disappeared with them.

My father had taken me to another fancy restaurant to celebrate my starting high school, but once I was in college, I never heard from him again. My mother was always telling me that the older I got, the more I took after him. Of course, she only said that when she was mad at me. She stopped talking about him after I started college. I guess, since I was grown up, she finally came to terms with the fact that he'd left. Though she looked much freer than before, that didn't necessarily mean she was happy. Maybe she'd taken too long getting there. "Now that you're in college, you have to start taking care of your mother." Had I seen my father then, I'm sure that's what he would have said. Saying that was pretty much the only thing he could do for her.

Phone Call on a Sunday

MY THIRTY-FIFTH BIRTHDAY fell on a Sunday. After church, my mother prepared the traditional birthday soup made with dried seaweed, which she'd soaked in water the night before. Watching television with her after she finished washing the dishes, I declared that I was going on a diet in honor of my birthday. She stared at me dubiously, as if she'd just heard those words from a bear preparing to hibernate. I'd been fat my entire life, ever since I was a baby. It wasn't easy, of course, but in order to love yourself, you'll adapt to any condition, no matter how bad, and find ways to rationalize it. Since Mom had spent the last thirty-something years assuming that I was okay with being obese, I understood why she looked at me like that. But she didn't seem to pick up on why I'd suddenly decided to go on a diet.

"It'll be nice to have more room on the drying rack," she said tentatively.

She'd always complained that there wasn't enough space on the rack to hang all the laundry, even though it was only the two of us, because my clothes were so huge. It never occurred to her that maybe she just needed to do the laundry more often.

"Hmm, I wonder if the house'll feel bigger too," she added, looking around at the room, her tired, expressionless face hardened from the passing of time.

A talk show was re-airing on a cable station. As the faces of the program guests appeared on the screen, my mother moved closer to the TV set. Two attractive young men dressed like twins in identical white clothing appeared, shaking their long, feathered hair and smiling sweetly too much. She'd never even heard their music, but they had recently become her favorite celebrities. Each time she saw them on TV, she asked without fail, "Which one is Hyeonjung, and which is Hyeongjun?" She had no idea whether I was giving her the right answer, but she could always tell when I wasn't sure. Not that she really expected a sincere response from me. She had long ago gotten into the habit of talking to herself as if we were having a conversation, having realized that no amount of complaining would change my terse personality. "It'd be easier to tell them apart if there were three of them, but it's harder when there's only two. Like telling a left turn from a right turn." That spring my mother had given up on trying to get a driver's license after she had failed the written test for the eighth time. She must have been thinking that once she gave up on trying to tell Hyeonjung from Hyeongjun, she may as well start giving up on more and more things in her old age.

After attending a two-hour lecture to the effect that growing old was a matter of learning the composure needed to accept and resign oneself to senility, she stopped going to the Senior Citizen's Welfare Center. Although she had been forced to give up many things in the course of her life, what she hated most was resignation and feeling pressured to resign oneself to something. In actual fact—and you can call it resignation if you like—my mother never really got to make any of her own choices. Including when she held me in her arms for the first time.

When the program ended, she sat back from the TV and asked me, "How many kilograms are you going to lose?" When I said I planned to lose twenty, she cocked her head and nodded again. As I went back into my room, she muttered, "Are you hoping to meet someone?" Though she liked to complain that I was impossible to figure out, I sometimes thought there was nothing she didn't know about me. This was one of those times.

Of course, it's not that I had never thought about dieting until now. You can't ignore what's going on in the world. Nowadays, fat people aren't just seen as dopey and apathetic. They're also treated like lazy good-for-nothings who lack self-control and don't take care of themselves. I knew full well that the many blind dates I'd been set up with, and undoubtedly my own mother as well, probably thought at some point that my abilities in bed would leave a lot to be desired. My friend B joked that if I went over a hundred kilograms, I'd have to start calculating my weight in tons. "'0.1' looks better and sounds more aspirational than '100.' To be honest, if it weren't for your weight, you'd be far too average in every way." I don't know if it was because I was a stubborn fat kid at heart (as B always claimed), or if after all I was anything but average, but I hated being manipulated by conformist values. The only thing that could influence me was certain people who were important to me.

That afternoon, I took the bus and went to a large bookstore in the Gwanghwamun district of Seoul. After poring through dozens of books for about two hours, I bought three diet books that I thought sounded more convincing than the others. B's company, which closed on Saturdays and opened on Sundays instead, was ten minutes away. B answered his phone immediately. I told him I'd come out to buy some books, and he assured me he'd be there before I'd read even two pages. However, it was two hours before he showed up. A newspaper reporter is like an alcoholic husband: he always has a perfectly logical excuse for being late and never fails to add that he's going on the wagon for real this time. While talking to me, he read the titles of the books next to me, simultaneously going over the day's lead stories in his head.

According to B, it would be like living a new life. I'd never again suffer the indignity of having someone in a crowded elevator hit the close button as I came rushing up, gasping for air, about to set one foot inside. And I'd be freed from turning red in the face whenever I tied my shoes, worrying that I might unwittingly strain too hard and let out a fart. I'd leave behind the anguish of concealing my wounded pride whenever a waitress mistakenly delivered a meal I'd ordered to some extremely ugly, sloppily dressed fatso—since all fat people look alike—and having to call her over in a loud voice. "That's right," B said. "All of us, including you, will finally get a look at the real you, the you that's been wrapped up inside those rolls of flesh." B considered it entirely my fault that his old car had lost its muffler. "Don't you realize that the bottom of the car sinks so low when you're in it that I can barely make it over the speed bumps? From now on, whenever you get on an airplane or boat or roller coaster, or whatever, you won't have to worry whether the person next to you is wondering if it's going to tip over." Ordering one last bottle of soju, B asked, "Why did you decide to lose weight all of a sudden, anyway? Trying to get laid?"

The question was inspired by a recent reunion of high school friends whom I hadn't seen in years. One of the guys bragged about how he used his corporate card to hit the hottest spots in Gangnam and enjoy unlimited one-night stands. Married friends responded nonchalantly to his bragging, but the unmarried ones gradually leaned in closer. When his entertaining tales of adventures with women at the company's expense ended, one of the guys sighed deeply. "I haven't gotten laid in eleven months, three weeks, and two days." "What?" "No way!" An exaggerated chorus of sighs arose all around, as if they were a paid audience filling the studio seats for a talk show. On the way home afterward, I confided to B that it had been two years more for me than for that friend. I only brought it up—parroting the way he had recited the months, weeks, and days—to joke that he must've been keeping a daily tab if he knew the number so precisely, but B misunderstood. "Honestly, I don't think dieting's going to fix that for you," B said, looking all too serious. "The problem is you have to be more assertive. When's the last time you simply approached a woman and tried striking up a conversation?" We'd known each other so long, but there was still so much that B didn't know about me. I wasn't passive about wanting things. It's just that I'd lived my whole life having to always consider first whether it was okay for me to want something before I *started* wanting it. And besides, I didn't need B to tell me that, when it came to getting laid, there were plenty of easier ways to make that happen than going on a diet. I wasn't that stupid.

By the time we left the bar, night had already fallen and was waiting for us.

"How's your mother?" B walked with me to the bus stop after he'd called for someone to drive him home. "Has she been bored since selling the restaurant?"

"She's taking it easy. I think she goes there sometimes to eat. She taught the new owner her recipes, so the food still tastes like hers."

Actually that was the excuse she gave. She had to be bored to death after twenty years of the same food, always in the same place, but she had nowhere else to go.

"Is she still going to the same church?"

"No, she switched to the Full Gospel Church. She said she couldn't stand watching those stuck-up Gangnam wives puckering their lips like goldfish each time they sang, so she switched to a church where she can bawl out hymns at the top of her lungs."

"Your mother is so feisty." B laughed loudly.

Since it was a Sunday evening, the bus wasn't too crowded. As I placed my new books on the empty seat next to mine, B's words came to mind. It was true that every time I took a seat on a bus, I was careful not to touch the person sitting next to me. Several times I'd been unable to bear the misunderstanding of some young woman and got off the bus before my stop. I smiled wryly. B was different from me in every way. I was unnecessarily complicated and sensitive; he was simple, cheerful and devoid of malice, befitting a son brought up in a loving environment. I didn't know him as a child, but he must have looked so bright and innocent.

I turned to gaze out the window. The road outside was darker than usual. There weren't many cars; the streetlights traced patterns across the dark asphalt. My mother had always wanted to change her boring life but was never able to. The only thing she could change was the church she attended. She'd never been a feisty person with a stomach for drama. In fact, had she answered the phone call that morning, she might well have replied flatly that it was the wrong number, that the person they were looking for didn't live there. But then, not only would her hands have been shaking too hard for her to prepare lunch, she'd have been unable to look me in the eye when I asked who called and would've gone to bed early to avoid answering me.

I'd gotten the call a week ago while she was at church. It was a young man. He said he got the number from the restaurant, and asked whether he was correct in assuming that I was the son. Then he mentioned my father's name and told me the name of the hospital and the room number. It was a short conversation. It was thanks to a kindly nurse on duty at the hospital that I learned what was wrong and when they were planning to operate.

"Are you family?"

"Yes, I am," I answered drily, like the young man who had phoned.

A week went by, and the only thing I did was call up the restaurant to tell them to stop giving out our number to strangers. I asked them not to tell my mother that someone had called there looking for us. I tried to remember what my father looked like, but I drew a blank. Instead, what I pictured was a fat kid, lost in sad thoughts, hurrying after his father for fear of losing him.

Our Daily Bread

DR. ROBERT ATKINS, a cardiologist, discovered an interesting fact while performing autopsies on deceased soldiers during the Vietnam War. Thick slabs of fat were attached to their internal organs. These layers of fat were common in older people who eat too much meat and don't get enough exercise, but what were they doing in young soldiers in combat? It was due to carbohydrates, the staple of their diet. The human body is one big chemical factory. Excess carbohydrates in the body turn to fat, but fat, no matter how much is consumed, can't be stored without carbohydrates. That's where the theory of the Atkins Diet comes from—eat all the fat you want but no carbohydrates.

My mother, who had run a small restaurant that served rice soup for over twenty years, naturally held the opposite theory. When I told her that I'd lose weight by eating pork belly, she was dumbfounded and asked where all that grease would go. I tried telling her that once food enters the body, it metabolizes into different substances, but it was no use. She was especially unyielding when I said I'd completely cut out carbohydrates like rice, bread, noodles, and rice cakes. She insisted that rice was healthy, homegrown produce eaten by generation after generation of our ancestors, and that noodles contain only half the calories of rice, while buckwheat noodles are widely known as a diet food. She had been watching daytime TV almost every day without fail. When I told her I couldn't eat fruit or drink juice either, she retorted, "Even sugar-free juice?"

"Fruit is high in sugar. And don't buy potatoes, either. Starch immediately breaks down into carbohydrates."

She raised her eyebrows, full of confidence. "Can you name one food that's as nutritious as a potato?"

"Yeah, yeah, I know," I said, trying to cut her off, as I wasn't accustomed to explaining things to her. Everyone knows how much sugar and potatoes have contributed to human history. The problem is that this is no longer an era of nutritional deficiency when people need to generate energy at low cost. On the contrary, this is an era in which, in the U.S. alone, billions of dollars are spent every year on dieting and keeping in shape.

The scale I'd ordered online arrived the following day. People think the hardest things fat people have to deal with are struggling to walk upstairs or spending too much money on food, but that's not true. What's far more uncomfortable is the fact that we can't do anything without being noticed. One of the major advantages of online shopping is that, just as a bachelor can quietly purchase a blow-up doll, a fat person can shop for extra-large clothes or a scale without feeling like everyone is staring at them. Standing on the first scale I'd ever owned in my life, I gazed down at the needle as it sped blithely past the numbers. Later that day, I bought a small spiral-bound notebook with pages ruled in blue from the stationery store next to the bus stop. The notebook was held closed by a fabric-covered rubber band and contained fifty pages. I tore out eight of the pages and numbered the remaining forty-two, one for each day of my diet. My preparations were pretty much complete.

The Second Week

I STARTED THE first day by recording my weight.

For breakfast I ate vegetables with either eggs or tofu. I had to change my entire cooking style to be able to eat without getting bored. For vegetables, I alternated between tomatoes, cucumbers, and bell peppers. Dinner was meat or fish. I ate grilled pork one day and sushi the next, followed by grilled fish, fried bacon, boiled chicken, grilled sirloin, and so on. From anyone's point of view, they were decent meals to be sure, but it took more patience than I thought to eat the same food every day. It was a particular struggle to eat all of these things without rice. Up until then, I'd always chosen my meals based on the main items and thought of rice as something that automatically came with them. Now it was completely different. My appetite demanded only rice, and just the thought of that warm, glossy rice sent my body into a frenzy. It wasn't simply because I liked rice. The body can only store fat if carbohydrates are consumed with it. So my body's instinct was to plead and clamor for carbohydrates.

Lunch was the hardest. I offended the restaurant owner by eating only side dishes, not even touching the rice. I ordered plates of dumplings and left the peeled dumpling skins behind. When I ordered bibimbap, I skimmed off the hot pepper paste, which contained added sugar and glutinous rice powder, and ate the vegetables on top without mixing them into the rice underneath.

When I ate out with coworkers, they'd talk through the entire meal about the fact that I'd started dieting, the incomprehensible aspects of the diet I'd chosen, and all the terrible things that everyone knew would happen to someone as fat as me if I didn't go on a diet. One guy who'd joined the company the same year as me made the most scathing comments regarding the side effects of dieting and the yo-yo syndrome, feigning friendly concern. The only one among them who didn't speak was the new female employee, but I could sense that she was using her chopsticks quietly so as to not miss a single word. It was all outward encouragement. But I didn't enjoy the attention, knowing I was only this week's gossip. Eventually, I started eating out alone. I pushed all my dinner dates back six weeks.

I started noticing changes in my body after three days. I felt dizzy, like I'd become anemic, and had trouble concentrating. Whenever I saw a chair, I sank into it even if only for a short while. I lost enthusiasm for everything, and even my daily routine at the office became difficult for me to handle. When the new female employee overtook me as I was walking slowly up the stairs holding onto the handrail, she carried my files for me like she couldn't just stand by and watch.

"Are you okay? You look pale."

I hated the fact that I was drawing attention to myself, but I pointed at my head and smiled wryly.

"My brain is angry with me."

"What? What about your brain?"

Since I didn't have the energy to explain further, her wide, innocent-looking eyes began to grate on my nerves. The brain, the most sophisticated part of our body, doesn't bother with tedious tasks. Instead of producing energy for its own use, it gets its supply of glucose from carbohydrates, but recently it had been getting none. Dr. Atkins said you shouldn't satisfy your brain's demands. Over time, the brain can't help but adapt to the new system. However, you clearly risk a certain degree of danger by not feeding your brain, even for a short time.

My mother, of course, noticed the change in me. On the fifth day of my diet, she tried to serve me samgyetang, a soup made from a whole spring chicken and medicinal herbs.

"You can eat chicken, right?"

She tried to sound nonchalant, as if no one had ever told her that the chicken in samgyetang was stuffed with sweet, glutinous rice. I, in turn, was speechless, unable to do anything but stare blankly at the chicken, the steam trailing off of it, the savory aroma of cooked rice. Yes, I could eat meat, but the instant I chased it with a spoon of rice or a bite of noodles, I would start gaining weight—this explanation was so patently obvious that it refused to leave my lips. Instead, my mouth pooled with saliva. While I hesitated, my selfish, greedy body had already tucked in the napkin, and was sitting there holding a knife and fork, looking at me with an expression that said: Come on, hurry up.

"People have to eat grains to stay healthy."

As she stared at me, my mother's words were so terribly tempting. She wasn't wrong. You only had to picture a farmer's rice bowl mounded high like a grave to realize it: next to sugar, grains are the food most easily converted into energy. But in my state, forced to burn up all my surplus reserves, I absolutely had to avoid consuming any.

After a light meal of canned tuna and tofu for dinner, I had an unpleasant taste in my mouth, so my mother brought me fragrant honeyed water in a clear glass with ice cubes floating in it. "It's the only way. Listening to your body is the key to health." Her words, as sweet as the honeyed water, were also true. Like a baseball coach, the body sends us all kinds of signals to control the game called survival. The problem is that when it comes to fat, there is an absolute difference between the satisfaction my body craves and the health I desire. As for my brain, it was increasingly not on my side. My brain was the one ordering my stomach to stock up on glucose in order to secure energy for itself, regardless of what damage it did to my other organs. Frantic to go on storing more, the brain is always three minutes late in telling the body that the stomach is full. Even as I reluctantly waved away the honeyed water, I could feel at the same time someone inside of me struggling desperately to get out, one shoe dangling off in his haste, to grab the glass from her.

The grilled mackerel and pan-fried tofu that I'd asked her to make were served for dinner the next day. But there was also a bowl of glossy rice and fried squid with noodles on top, which I hadn't asked for. Everything was in very small portions. My mother declared that everyone knows it's bad to eat an unbalanced diet, and she ordered me to eat a variety of foods but to stick to half-size servings of each, just as the daytime talk show host advised. I ignored her, so she changed her tactics again the next day. In addition to salt and pepper, she used a sweet marinade for the meat, and she even added sugar, which was pure carbohydrates, to spicy chicken soup and fried squid. The less I was able to overcome temptation, the bigger my discontent with her grew. Eventually, I started losing my temper at the table.

It began with me shouting that she had to discard her old-fashioned ideas about food and other things. I grumbled that she should let me handle my problems my own way, especially when it came to my own body. But the grumbling grew into nervous criticism. I even told her bluntly that I'd never be able to get married, as she so desired, if I failed this diet, and would therefore never give her any grandchildren, who were obviously bound to have been fat themselves. I implied that her current, hopeless life was fate's inevitable revenge for her one immoral act. I knew exactly how to hurt her. But my mother had enough dignity to despise those who hurt her. Whenever she couldn't get her way, she reminded me of her absolute authority and self-sacrifice on my behalf when I was just a helpless, wretchedly abandoned unborn child, and she did so with enough force to stuff me back into her womb like a boa constrictor swallowing an elephant.

"Why did you give birth to me?"

"Why did I have a son like you?"

Had we been a chicken and an egg, we still would have growled at each other like this.

The diet was difficult because I had to struggle against the

millennia-old system of survival instincts built in to my body.
Ever since the Stone Age, the human body has been programmed
to store fat. But today's standards of beauty and health call for
burning off all of one's body fat. Dieting creates a dilemma
between our primitive body and modern culture. That dilemma
confronted me daily, testing me at every corner of my life. One
day, upon returning to my desk, I found a paper plate with a
slice of mousse cake topped with sweetened whipped cream and
a bright red strawberry waiting for me. A cup of soda sat beside
it. A co-worker, whipped cream already stuck to the corners of
his mouth, waved a fork as he told me it was the new female
employee's birthday. I sensed all my coworkers watching the
plate and me, as if they'd placed bets.

"Have mine, too." I moved the plate to my colleague's desk.
Looking intrigued as I handed him the soda as well, he playfully
quizzed me.

"Why is soda bad for you?"

"Eating sugar and fat at the same time makes your body
store the fat." I kept my voice slow and calm. "If you wonder
why bad things taste so good, it's because you have the body
of a millennia-old primitive man who goes crazy at the mere
mention of fat."

I called the other person living inside my body Primitive
Man. I started feeling hostile toward the animal instinct for
survival and the way my body was programmed to cling to
its instincts. Human beings don't have sex just to preserve the
species anymore. My birth was proof enough of that. And yet,
my body's programming insists that I am an animal no different from Ice Age man. Why is it that hedonistic humans have
resisted the instinct to preserve the species but still submit to the
pleasure of instinctively storing fat? Is that our dominant gene?
Seeking out pleasure?

The weight came off little by little. There were days when I
weighed the same as before, but even on those days, my body felt
lighter. My watch hung loose on my wrist, and I had to tighten

my belt by three notches. While buttoning my collar, I discovered that my weight loss had started in my neck. When I glanced at my reflection in the mirror while taking a shower, it seemed as though there was more space in the mirror, and when I bumped into someone in a narrow hallway, I only had to turn slightly to get past them without touching the wall. Even catching cabs became easier. There were more and more instances in which the new female employee, who had previously been so hesitant to respond whenever I pointed something out, smiled and replied promptly. Once I'd lost eight kilograms, I became convinced that this diet was proof that modern humanity represented a new stage of existence, having abandoned the natural choices made by animals for the choices of enlightened civilization. But more importantly, I found satisfaction in the thought that I was resisting my genetic inheritance. In the meantime, three weeks passed.

Things You Can Choose and Things You Can't

B MET ME at work for lunch one day.

"You can eat everything but carbs, right? Doesn't seem that hard."

But B and I had to keep passing up restaurants. Ox bone soup, hangover soup, sushi, fried rice, curry—these foods are unimaginable without rice. Even light noodle soups like *naeng-myeon* and *udon* are nothing but carbohydrates. Same for pasta. B stopped in front of a Chinese restaurant.

"They serve meat."

"Yeah, but Chinese food is full of starch."

Standing on the sidewalk and looking at the signboards of restaurants around him, B's gaze settled without much hope on a sandwich shop across the street.

"I guess that won't work either."

"Bread is bad enough, but mayonnaise has sugar in it."

"Well, I don't care if you eat or not, I got to have something." Complaining that he was losing his appetite, B finally hauled me into the nearest fast food restaurant.

B ordered fried chicken, a soda, and a biscuit, and I ordered a burger without any sauce.

"Aren't you going to end up malnourished if you keep skipping rice?" he asked. "Seems to me that diets work by forcing you to lose weight through malnutrition."

Since every person who talked to me over the past few weeks had questioned me about diets, I was sick of the subject, but I tried explaining that dieting is more a matter of metabolism than calories: Though lions eat only meat, they don't have problems with their nutritional balance because they synthesize carbohydrates inside their bodies. On the contrary, even though cows eat only grass, they have a lot of fat. Camels hold fat in their humps and are able to cross the desert because that fat converts into water when it burns.

B snickered. "Listen to you! You sound like a broken record."

A boy waiting for his mother who'd gone to order was sitting by himself across from me and staring hard at me. I don't like fast food places, and it's not just because whenever a fat person appears, people immediately think of lawsuits against McDonald's. It's also because people can see up close what others are eating, and because those places are usually full of children. Young children, being candid, stare openly at whomever catches their eye, and most parents, acknowledging only their children's right to innocence, fail to teach them about respecting others who don't wish to be stared at. If they see me eating just a salad, the parents will whisper to their child, "He has to watch what he eats because he's fat. But he's still fat even though he eats so little. Don't you feel sorry for him?" And yet, if I'm eating french fries, a double burger, and a coke, they don't automatically look the other way because it makes sense for my size. They give each other looks that say, "That's why he's fat," and try to stifle their laughter, then quickly look away when they feel me looking at them. Fat people don't stick out because we're big. We get stared at because people feel there's something different about us. The boy watched closely as I ate the insides of the burger and tossed the buns onto the tray.

B pointed at the chicken. "Want some? You said you can eat fatty food."

"Plain chicken is okay," I said, "but that looks like it dove into the fryer wearing a cheap coat."

B raised one eyebrow and gave me a bitter look "This is a real struggle for you," he said.

"Yeah, I envy bears the most. They lose weight just by sleeping all winter."

"They lose weight in their sleep?" He laughed. "Never knew bears got liposuction."

"No kidding," I said. "Nice to know they can afford it."

But B didn't look like he was enjoying joking around as usual. I could hear the ice rattling as B absentmindedly shook his cup. I changed the topic.

"Do you know why people overeat?" I asked, and launched into another lecture.

Back in the Ice Age, our ancestors starved on a regular basis. Many died because they couldn't make it through the lean times when there were no plants to gather or animals to hunt. Therefore, if they did find something to eat after all that waiting, they would throw a big feast and overeat. The purpose of the feast was to store fat, and the purpose of storing fat was to be able to survive the next cold spell, drought, or other lean season. If children don't eat properly for even a week, their limbs stop growing. According to researchers who study the bones and teeth of prehistoric humans, there is a clear difference in density between the parts that stopped developing due to starvation and the parts that developed actively after a round of heavy eating. The ability to survive didn't depend simply on eating but on overeating. Therefore, even fat people, whose bodies have more than enough fat stored for emergencies, still get hungry and crave the taste of food regularly. Overeating is a genetic flaw built into the human body.

"In other words, all you have to do is blame everything on your ancestors," B interrupted me.

Strangely enough, the look on his face as he stared at me was identical to the look on the face of the kid sitting across the way. It was the first time B had ever looked at me like I was fat. His expression seemed to say that, while trying to fight my inner fat guy, I end up becoming the fat guy.

"What you're saying," B added, his face still that of a stranger, "is that it's not your fault because you were born this way. Am I right?"

I put the empty cup and dirty napkins on the tray without a word. He went on.

"You seem to really hate the guy you call 'Primitive Man,' but aren't you the one crying out for fat? You think you're a highly rational being in command of yourself while he's a primitive barbarian living off of you like a parasite? Bullshit. He existed long before you got this shell you call your 'body.' He is you. Isn't that right?"

I picked up the tray and got up without responding. The innocent, well-adjusted kids never understand. They don't get why the dumb, grouchy-looking fat kids don't join them at recess but instead watch them from behind the classroom window, a candy bar clutched greedily in each hand, a ring of chocolate around their mouths, the sweetness, the animosity. Goddammit! Who cares whose genes are inside my body?

At The Dinner Table

THAT EVENING, I returned home and ate grilled pork belly with half a bottle of soju. I usually drank beer, but I took Dr. Atkin's advice and chose soju instead. My mother drank the other half. The TV was on behind me. Her eyes were glued to Hyeon-jung and Hyeong-jun.

"Tell me the truth," she said. "Why are you suddenly so crazy about losing weight? What's going on?"

I looked down at the sliced pork belly cooking on the electric pan. She'd separated the fat from the lean, and a bit of leftover fat was sizzling especially loudly. Holding the last shot of soju, I glanced up out of habit at the wall behind her. There was nothing hanging on it.

It had been two weeks since his operation, so I thought he'd be out of the hospital by then. But the patient was still in his hospital room, awaiting a second operation. I'd wanted to ask how he was but I hung up the phone instead. I didn't want even the nurse to know that I was curious. I hid my desire to know whether the patient wanted to see me. I didn't even ask if he was in pain. It's not that I didn't care, but the years had built up between us, like cholesterol thickening the blood, and I could not just feel bad for him.

I opened my notebook and was checking the dates when my mother shrieked.

"You're not blocking the TV anymore! Hyeon-jung came on alone this time, right?"

I moved aside so she could see the rest of the screen. She joked a lot when she got tipsy. On TV, handsome young men were grimacing and eating rice cakes stuffed with horseradish as a penalty for losing a game.

"Good-looking people look good even when they're eating." She was talking to herself again. "They say when you get old, you look ugly when you eat. Who wants to look at something ugly? That's when it's time to take a person's food away. Time for them to die. They say that's what happens when you stop loving someone. When love cools, the thing you hate the most is watching them eat. Wanting to take someone's food away . . . I guess that's the same as wanting them to die, huh? There's nothing more vulgar than eating. They say you first fall for someone while eating together, and that love grows at the table."

"If you look pretty when you eat, you'll turn into a pig," I remarked cynically.

She stopped wiping the grease from the pan and heaved a deep sigh.

"Why don't you go buy another bottle of soju," she said, throwing down the greasy paper towel. "You claim to be losing weight but you never exercise. And stop acting like rice is your mortal enemy."

The more she drank, the more her jokes turned into nagging, and then to sob stories about her sorry life.

"You shouldn't do that," she said. "It wasn't that long ago that there simply wasn't enough to eat. Everyone went hungry in spring waiting for the barley to ripen. Back then, you did whatever you had to not to starve. Do you have any idea how many families in our neighborhood sent their daughters to work nights in seedy bars just so they could eat?" .

"Times have changed," I said, cutting her off. "No one starves to death nowadays, so you—"

I gulped down what I wanted to say next because she was glaring at me. Even after I stopped talking, she kept staring hard at me. She looked both mystified and dubious.

"What?" I asked bluntly, and she laughed and shook her head.

"Nothing, you just reminded me of someone."

The Final Week

MY BODY SEEMED to have completely shifted from synthesizing fat to burning fat. I got my rhythm back, and could tell from the astonished looks on everyone's faces that the changes to my body had become noticeable. When a client I hadn't seen in a while dropped by and said he almost didn't recognize me, the new female employee chimed in and said, "Isn't he incredible?" Then she turned to me and added, "I never noticed how big your eyes are." With each step, I could tell that my butt had grown smaller. My footsteps felt much lighter, and the loss of my double chin made nodding effortless. "So, this is how you become a positive person," I murmured in front of the mirror.

My colleague congratulated me on my shrinking belly. He even asked me whether his potbelly had anything to do with the fact that each time he hiked, he grabbed wildly at trees and rocks rather than tightening his stomach muscles. I explained that since most fat is stored in the belly, the body defends it to the end, making belly fat the last to go. The new female employee asked me why sweet foods were fattening. I told her that the quickest source of energy is an injection of glucose. The next quickest is sweet foods. Since it only takes a single step to convert sugary foods into glucose, the body naturally hungers for sweets when it's tired. Newborn babies are born already craving sweetness and will seek out their mother's milk, which contains sugar, and thus survive. Likewise, children, who need a lot of calories to grow, can't help liking sweets. The reason old people crave sweets is a little different. My mother, who could finish off an entire bowl of sweet-and-sour pork by herself, used to rationalize her gluttony by saying, "You revert back to child-hood as you grow old," as if it were some tried and true proverb. But unlike children, old people don't need that many calories. Instead, eating sweets is a way for the aged body, having grown weak and wily and disinclined to work too hard, to get energy quickly and easily.

My physical changes weren't the only thing. Fat people's larger frames tend to make their feet look disproportionately small and sad, but now I felt like my silhouette had come alive. My suit jackets that used to strain against my arms and back to the point of tearing at the seams were now much looser. Fortunately, all the stores were holding sales just then. I bought two suits and a brightly colored spring shirt. I felt lighthearted, as if the world were opening up before me.

I called the hospital for the third time, my fingers in a rush to dial, only to learn that the second operation hadn't gone well. The nurse, speaking in the same kind tone, told me to contact the hospital's funeral parlor. I dialed again, this time trembling. The funeral was the next day.

I returned home and hung my new suits in the closet. They had an air of politeness and dignity, their shoulders bowed forward slightly like they were entering someone else's house, so different from the tired clothes that had been there so long. Exuding luster and a sense of vigor, like junior staff with innovative plans, the suits dispelled the air of gloom that had settled in my long unchanging wardrobe. My gaze stopped at the sight of my old jacket hanging in the far corner. Unlike my perky new clothes, the arms sagged like a shed skin and the voluminous space between the back of the jacket and the front lapels looked sad and empty, as it nothing could ever fill it. I took the jacket out and slowly brushed it with a lint roller. It was the only black suit I owned. I could hear my mother talking to herself in the kitchen as she set the table for dinner. She was probably grumbling about the dishes I'd requested. As I listened, I felt a sorrow more excruciating than any I'd ever felt in my life.

Children Born by Accident

BACK WHEN WE were kids, B used to joke that he was born by accident.

"I would never have been born if my dad either didn't have five thousand won for a motel room or did have fifty thousand won for an abortion."

But B's story changed each time he told it.

"Actually, my dad did give my mom money for an abortion. But on the way to the clinic, she was passing in front of a store where a beaded purse in the window caught her eye. My mom blew all the money for the abortion on a purse. Her motto for everything is 'I'll deal with it later.' That's her style. Otherwise, I wouldn't be here. Anyway, that's what happened. I competed against a beaded purse and lost, and that's how my life began."

Some days, B changed his story from the purse to a pleated skirt or a pearl ring. I envied the way he could joke about how he was born.

We were nearly thirty when B told me what had really happened.

"The truth is, I used to have an older sister."

B's parents had one son and one daughter, so I already knew B had a big sister, three years older than him.

"I'm not talking about her. I mean the one who was born the year before me. She's still my sister, even if she did die four months after she was born."

B's father was the only son born in his family for two generations; therefore, it was his duty to pass on the family name. From the day their first daughter was born, the family elders started pressuring B's father to have a son. Two years later, when his wife became pregnant again, B's grandfather didn't even consider the other possibility and prepared five potential boys' names based on their family tree. But, just like the last time, it was a girl. B's father would come home from work every night to find his wife crying under the blankets, holding the newborn. One day, when the baby was three months old and B's mother was feeling better, she put the baby down for a nap and took her older daughter with her next door to visit their neighbor. When she returned, the baby was dead, face down with her little nose and mouth buried in the blanket. B's father despaired. Just the day before, he'd secretly had a vasectomy. He thought it was the best solution to his family's irrational expectations, which even he thought were crazy. He didn't want to impose those expectations on his wife after her second pregnancy had left her so depressed. But while he had accepted the idea of raising two daughters, he hadn't planned on raising an only child. Back to the hospital he went. The doctor told him some sperm could still be alive inside his body, so they might still conceive, though the chances were low. Immediately after burying their second daughter, the couple jumped into bed. To their surprise, she got pregnant again and gave birth to a baby the following year. This time it was a boy.

B said he'd never forget the shock of hearing his grandfather, who loved his grandson exclusively and believed that girls had no souls, describe it as the time the family narrowly escaped disaster. It wasn't until much later that B became both repulsed and fascinated—by the remarkable determination of the sperm that bore his name and that stayed alive in his father's scrotum for over three days before emerging into the world and succeeding at its task, by the way his newborn older sister had made the entire family happy by breathing her last feeble breath just a hundred days after her birth, by the selfish, merciless family instinct that, in the end, whether anyone had intended it or not, conspired to commit murder, and by the bargain, swiftly made, to exchange death for life. To him, his parents were no better than chimpanzees—the female lewdly shaking her red, swollen genitals, and the male running after her, grunting, nose aquiver. Had his mother really lingered so long at the neighbor's with no ulterior motive? He had his doubts about all of it, but what troubled B the most in his adolescence was the sense of disillusionment he felt toward his father's desires. How had his father been capable of shuddering in sexual pleasure on the very blanket where his newborn baby's corpse had lay? The only way B could endure it was by cracking jokes about his own birth.

B's last words that day were still clear in my mind. "I think I've come to terms with it now. Life goes on, mean and dirty, and that's how we learn about the world—through our fathers' hypocrisy."

"Maybe," I replied coolly. "But it's different for you and me. Your dad went back to the doctor so he could have you. My father never wanted me at all."

Venus

I DIDN'T HAVE the courage to go in and pay my respects before my father's photo. I formally presented my condolence money at the entrance, took a step back behind the other funeral guests who were just then arriving, and retreated to the hallway. A young man dressed in black came up to me with a friendly look on his face. I reluctantly let him lead me into the crowded room where people were eating. No one took any notice of me. Of course, it wasn't the sort of place where people show curiosity toward others, but then I realized that I was no longer so fat as to be conspicuous. I thought I'd just sit near the entrance briefly and leave right away, but the young man in charge of the funeral arrangements politely asked me to sit further inside. There was an empty seat in the far corner. I sat and stared blankly for a moment at the liquor bottles and food that were set out on the table.

A middle-aged woman with a white pin in her hair came to me carrying a bowl of soup on a tray. She set the bowl in front of me and gave me a friendly look; the whites of her eyes were bloodshot. I assumed she was related to the deceased.

"Have some soup and rice," she said. "It'll warm you up."

The spicy aroma pricked at my nose, while the white grains of rice floating in the oily red broth already had me excited. But instead of picking up a spoon, I quickly opened a soju bottle so that the grief-stricken woman with her kindly air wouldn't feel embarrassed that I hadn't touched the food. Other guests kept coming in, making it awkward to get up, so I just went on drinking soju. The soup cooled quickly.

Almost all of the tables were filled except for mine and, as luck would have it, it seemed to be reserved for relatives. All my life, I'd had almost no relationship with any extended family members. Ever since I was young, my mother didn't like outings with her family, where they got together and attacked each other with unwanted advice. Here, my father's relatives greeted each other warmly, remarking on how long it had been, and after briefly shedding tears, set about sharing food and drink while talking loudly about all kinds of things. I'd always imagined the people of my father's world. All the adults would be dignified and warm-hearted, and the children would be innocent and bright. But these people who were gathered to mourn my father were just normal people, like everyone else I knew. The wrinkles on their faces evoked both joy and sorrow, and they had a weary look about them, like they led ordinary lives, finding comfort in the little things or putting on brave fronts, just like the rest of us. There were also quite a few fat people. Maybe that was why no one looked my way. It didn't matter. They didn't know me, and I didn't know them.

"Oh, why didn't you eat? It's all cold now." The same woman returned and brought me a fresh bowl of soup even though I told her it was okay. Judging from the way relatives were addressing her, she must have been a sister of the deceased. A young man sitting next to me offered me a drink. "Excuse me, but I'm not sure who you are . . ." Instead of giving an answer, I quickly emptied the shot glass and returned it to him, thinking it was time to get out of there. The man didn't ask any more questions. Instead, he pointed to the steaming hot bowl of rice soup. "It's okay. Please, go ahead and eat." He was probably pressing me to eat, I realized, because the sight of some unknown person drinking alone at a funeral, where friends and family come together, suggests some kind of problem. Besides, to anyone looking, I was drinking too fast. I didn't have the heart to continue refusing food or his kindness—he even went so far as to put a spoon in my hand—so I gave in and began eating.

I chewed a mouthful of rice and felt it slide down my throat. My body started cheering like crazy. My stomach danced, and my insides grew warm with pleasure. Here are those carbohydrates you've been wanting so badly. The spoon moved faster and faster. While gulping down the soup, I got a strange feeling. I felt like a father feeding his starving children, or even, a messiah saving a suffering body. I felt disembodied. Despair and an impulsive, self-destructive spite accelerated my movements. Like a true party crasher, I emptied the bowl in a flash, soup dribbling down the sides of my mouth. As soon as I swallowed the last drop and set the bowl down, the woman in the white mourning dress approached me and asked, as if she'd been watching the entire time: "Would you like another bowl? You had so much to drink." She was probably being nice to me because she didn't want some unknown drunk causing problems at the funeral, but I nodded happily, like a child eager for praise. I wolfed down the second bowl even faster than the first, slurping with exaggeration.

Back in the Stone Age, people were always hungry. So they diligently stored fat whenever they got the chance. The human body has not yet adjusted to modern life with its surplus of nutrients. But we will eventually evolve. After all, isn't it only human to keep pushing a rock up a hill even though we know it's bound to roll back down again the moment we reach the top? That's right. There's no hurry. It took us tens of thousands of years to figure out how to sharpen stone. Or we can look at it this way: You could find yourself shipwrecked, there could be a citywide power outage, you could be cut off from civilization by a blizzard and facing starvation—how will you survive if you have no fat stored in your body? In other words, our programming is still effective. There is no machine as honest and obedient as the body. I nodded deeply. I'd just lost twelve kilograms by not consuming any carbohydrates for an entire month. My body had kicked and struggled, determined not to submit to my will, but in the end it yielded the results I wanted. My body really was my own. All right, then. And now the Primitive Man in me was partying because word got out that rice was on the way. If I kept eating rice soup like this, my body would immediately start storing fat. And my mother and I would sit together again at a peaceful, loving meal table.

As I raised my head from the bowl of soup that I was devouring, someone called out loudly in my direction, "Hey, you must be the third son!" He had begun rising to his feet, while I sat bewildered. "When did you get back from the States? You're starting to look more and more like Uncle."

I denied it, and with soup still dribbling from my mouth, I dropped the spoon and staggered to my feet. At that moment the thought suddenly hit me that everyone there knew who I was. Feeling queasy and red in the face, I pushed my way through the crowd, came out into the hallway, and collapsed onto one of the plastic chairs neatly lined up along the wall. Through an open door, I glimpsed the room where the portrait of the deceased was enshrined; it was completely empty. Everyone must have gone to eat, because the family members were nowhere to be seen. I could just make out my father's photo inside. Staggering slightly, I went in to see what he had looked like as an old man.

Perhaps I'd kept looking at Botticelli's Venus that day to avoid seeing something else. Whenever things I didn't want to see rose again and again before my eyes, Venus intercepted them and took me to a door leading to someplace else. There, she told me the story of her birth. The youngest son of Uranus, the god of the sky, hid in his mother's genitals to cut his father's penis in half when it entered her, and then threw it into the sea. White froth gathered around it as it drifted in the current, and soon afterward a beautiful maiden was born in the foam, a goddess who would bring abundance and beauty to the world. But she couldn't free me from everything. In the end, the image remained: my younger self standing in front of a door that was always closed. In front of the door shut tightly against him, the fat boy took down his clumpy parka, which looked even shabbier for being the only one left on the coat stand, while outside the snow fluttered down.

At some point in my adolescence, another figure had begun to appear and disappear behind that picture. It was a naked women standing firmly on elephantine legs, her entire body wrapped in fat like a pelt. She was another goddess: the Venus of the Ice Age. Anthropologists say a woman that fat couldn't have actually existed at that time. Such a woman lived only in the imagination of the artist who created her. The artist of the Ice Age had imagined the most beautiful and voluptuous woman in the world, and she was the very picture of divine sustenance.

I saw the oldest son of the deceased walk into the room, preceded by two children dressed in black. When our eyes met, he bowed his head slightly in greeting as if he'd been waiting for me. With his hands on the shoulders of his two fat sons, he looked at me for a moment with a dignified air about him, not unlike my father had when he was younger. Our father's portrait hung behind him. Scowling at him, I walked resolutely towards the portrait. Just as I'd seen a world that differed from my own at that Italian restaurant, my father should also have seen a son who differed from what he knew. But he left with the memory of a fat kid. When I first saw Venus, I'd thought that everything beautiful in the world looked down me me. I bowed slowly before Father's portrait, rose, and turned my head to spit out an unchewed grain of rice. The queasiness rose up in my throat once more. Just then, the eldest son took a large picture frame that had been leaning against the wall hidden behind the funeral wreaths and handed it to me. The frame was meticulously covered in newspaper as if prepared with care in advance. It had been a long time, but the dimensions of the frame looked familiar. I didn't ask what it was.

Translated by Sora Kim-Russell

DISCOVERY OF SOLITUDE

1

WHEN I WAS little, I read a story once about a boy whose nose would grow longer with every lie he told. It's not like I believed every word of it, but afterwards, I couldn't bring myself to lie anymore. Lately I've begun to wonder: What if in that story, the boy would float into the air when he told a lie? Wouldn't I be a much better liar by now? And wouldn't I be living a much lighter existence? All that floating around might have given me a chance to see much more of the world.

It's possible that someone out there has already written that story. There are countless stories in this world, and nobody can actually read them all. I'd managed to turn thirty-eight without hearing most of the stories out there.

There was nothing special about my birthday. I was hanging around by myself in some secluded teahouse for hours on end. I must have refilled my cup of chamomile with hot water five, six times. I got myself real comfy on the couch and didn't budge except for trips to the bathroom. The book on the table remained face up, the pages unturned. I had nobody to see, nothing to do. More than that, I felt the distinct comfort of knowing there was nobody in the world who was thinking of me at that moment.

The last time I went home, Father had made a real effort to greet me warmly. He didn't nag me about choosing a different path for my life before it was too late. Father used to shower me with praise: I'd gotten honors for academic excllence and perfect attendance and was admitted into a prestigious university. In the end, though, studying was the only thing I knew how to do. This meant were I to fail at my studies, everything would be over for me. Father seemed to have more or less accepted this reality.

It wasn't anyone's fault. But something had gone wrong at some point. S used to get frustrated about how little I knew about the real world. Maybe this is the real world she was talking about.

I returned to my test prep dormitory a few days later, but I didn't resume my studies. When I caught myself compulsively checking my cell phone, I cancelled my service. It had rarely rung since S left me, and the only reason I'd kept it was probably so I could tell Father I was at the dorm if he called me to check. Even when I was out, I'd often hurry back to the dorm just so that I could give him that answer. The idea of lying hadn't even occurred to me.

The teahouse interior was cozy and quiet. As the February sun fell obliquely across the hardwood floor, the shadows from the blinds etched thin partitions of light across its planks. I was the sole customer. Behind the coffee machine on the counter, two waitresses in green aprons were making occasional small talk in a low whisper. I closed my eyes for a moment. A familiar tune drifted to my ears. It had been a long time since I'd listened to music. No one remembers your name. When you're strange, when you're strange, when you're strange . . . The dreamlike voice repeating these words tickled my ears like the sound of someone calling my name from a distance. Basking in the listless afternoon sun, I ended up dozing off.

I opened my eyes again at the sound of a small bell that rang whenever the door opened. I caught a glimpse of a tall man wearing a black coat who had just entered. The man was walking slowly toward where I was sitting. His movement seemed natural, as if he was supposed to meet me there, but I had no idea who he was.

The man was standing over me before I knew it. "You're K, aren't you?"

I nodded, signaling that I was indeed K. "Thanks," the man said and sat down across from me. It was as though he'd asked whether he could sit down and I had nodded yes. I looked blankly at the man as he took out a cigarette from his pocket and lit it silently. After taking a deep drag and exhaling smoke, he began to talk about the person I'd been fifteen years ago.

"Among the seven boys, K was definitely the model boarder. His fingernails and hair were always neatly trimmed, and not once was he late with the rent. Every semester, of course, he'd be awarded a scholarship.

"K never got mixed up in drinking sprees or late night rounds of *hwatu*[1] and he never had girls over to spend the night. He did laundry every Sunday so he always had clean underwear and socks in the drawers, and his was the only room in the entire house that didn't need to be tidied up in a hurry when parents showed up for a surprise visit. Furthermore, he spent most of his time at the boarding house at his desk studying. The housemother always placed the special dishes she prepared right in front of him, but each time, K would move the plate to the center of the table. Anyone could see after taking one look at him that he was a polite and wholesome young man. One with a bright and secure future ahead of him."

Until this man showed up, I had barely thought about this period of my life. I couldn't recall much of it either. But the more the man went on, the more certain I became that I was indeed the K in this story. I'd been living the same unchanged life, and tediously so; the only differences were that the boarding house fifteen years ago was now a test prep dorm. Back then, everyone had believed in me, even the housemother, but eventually my whole family grew sick of me.

I was startled by the shrill voice of a woman calling to the wait staff from her table by the entrance. This new customer must have come in while I'd been asleep. Why hadn't the bell rung when she entered? The woman had her hand above her

---

[1]   Hwatu: Korean playing cards.

eyes, shielding them from the sun with a furrowed brow. Several obsequious footsteps later the blinds snapped shut, illuminating the partitions of light that had stretched across the floor. The stark shadows cast on the man's face disappeared, and it became even harder to make out his expression.

The man leaned toward me and spoke in a secretive voice. I imagined a bank robber just out of prison asking about a former accomplice.

"I was wondering. Are you still carrying on with your research?"

I looked at him, perplexed.

He said with an unmistakably disappointed expression, "You know, the research on how to make yourself lighter?" The man went on. "We all believed that K could pull it off. He wasnt like the rest of us."

According to the man, the boarding house had been a two-story Western-style residence with six bedrooms. On the ground floor, there were two double rooms for boarders, in addition to the housemother's room. One of them was shared by two brothers in medical school who were very close. The other one belonged to a law student who was always complaining and a student majoring in management, who had only one outfit for every season of the year. The three rooms on the second floor were all singles. There was the only child from a wealthy family who was pretty good with the guitar and majoring in English. And there was the handsome engineering student who spent the night out most of the time. Then there was K. With the exception of the older guy taking classes at the medical school, somehow it turned out that all of the boarders had entered university the same year. They taped signs that read "Quiet" or "Please Knock Before Entering" on their identical-looking doors, and K's room was the second one at the top of the stairs, with a sign that read "DOORS."

The boarding house was in a neighborhood built on the side of a hill within the shadow of the mountains. It was always so windy, the boarders called it the "Windy Mountain." When the boarders spotted lovers outside the window on their way up the Windy Mountain, the boys would whistle and tease them playfully. K didn't whistle along with them, but he did enjoy looking out the window very much. The boarders often caught sight of K behind his brightly lit window while they were walking home late at night. Looking up the hill through the gusts of wind, the boarders always waved their hands in his direction, but it always took awhile before K's silhouette responded by calmly raising one hand. "He must have been deep in thought," the man added, "K knew everything that was going on in the boarding house."

No matter how hard I tried, I couldn't recall the K this man was describing. As for the habit of standing by the window, that hadn't changed. I still had a tendency to look out the window at night, and much like those days, I always felt something dark blocking my view. But it was only that I'd got tired of staring at books, not because I was searching for ways to make my body lighter than air. Moreover, it wasn't at all like me to be standing by the window watching for the other boarders coming home, since I'd never really taken an interest in other people's lives. His story became less and less believable. I began to lose interest.

"On days when the winds were particularly strong, it would carry what sounded like the cries of wild animals coming from the Windy Mountain. We all thought that K was doing an experiment trying to make himself lighter."

The man seemed to be caught in a pleasant memory; the corners of his mouth lifted to form a smile.

"I remember the day we all took a trip to an island. It was cold that day but fortunately the river hadn't frozen so we were able to get there by boat. I remember there was a temple at the center of the island . . ."

He shook his head in disappointment and said he couldn't remember the name of the temple.

"That night we thought K would share his research findings

with us. Even when the accident happened and the boat cap-
sized, we didn't think that K would sink. I remember how we
dried off in that *minbak*[2] house near the temple. I even remember how we went into the temple's main hall and lay down in
a neat row. We made some wonderful memories, wouldn't you
say?"

"The boarders must have gotten along well."

"Everyone liked K very much."

The man nodded a few times and looked straight at me as
though it was now my turn to speak.

"So how's everything these days, K?"

I don't know why, but it occurred me to say that I was getting
ready to pile up all those stupid books and set fire to my dorm
room. I actually did consider doing it once. Not setting the place
on fire, but telling a lie. That day, S hadn't acted irritable nor
had she unleashed her usual tirades on me. She'd seemed calm
the entire time, as though she'd given up any remaining hope
or interest in getting a rise out of me. "Making the decision was
hard, but actually going through with it, not really. What were
we thinking, letting this thing drag on for ten years?"

By the time we got to the bus stop, she was being particularly
cynical. "So you're just going to let me go. I knew you would
be like this. You're never going to change, so it's completely up
to me to decide whether I stay or leave, is that it? Fine, you're
right. Of course you can't promise me anything. Because when
have you ever been wrong? Good-bye."

During the bus ride back by myself, I thought carefully about
what she'd wanted from me. It occurred to me that she might
have wanted me to lie.

I looked straight into the man's eyes and answered him
plainly.

"I've been abroad all this time. My life's been too hectic. I'm
trying to figure out another way to be."

---

2   Minbak: A type of low-cost guesthouse, commonly run by
local families.

"I see."

"I might go live out in the country, where it's quiet."

"Is that right?"

The man lowered his gaze, as if deep in thought, and was silent for a while. Then he spoke again.

"Do you remember J, by any chance?"

Only when the man told me that J was the housemother's only son did the image of a short middle-schooler come to mind. He'd been a frighteningly quiet boy. The man said he was still in touch with J; that he'd even met up with the kid recently. Though he was all grown up now, J was still only as tall as a middle-schooler, but could definitely hold his own when it came to drinking.

"J is looking for someone to take over the inn."

"The inn?"

"Don't you remember? She stopped running the boarding house so that she could open the inn. That's why we had to move out of our beloved boarding house and go our separate ways."

The bridge of the man's nose wrinkled slightly when he said "beloved."

"After closing the boarding house, the housemother had spent the next few years running an inn down an alley in a college town. J was just about to turn twenty when the two of them relocated to W and took over another inn there. They were doing just enough business to get by. She passed away at the end of last year, though, only two months after getting diagnosed with late-stage throat cancer. The inn had yet to reopen after closing around the time of the funeral. J had no desire to operate an inn and wanted to sell it, but he wouldn't get a good price on the place if he left it vacant, so he'd been looking for someone to stay there for the time being. Now he was getting worried because the right person hadn't come along."

The man slowly removed a notebook and pen from inside his black coat and asked me for my address. The notebook looked brand new, with nothing written on it. The pen looked new as well. His handwriting was childish and crude like the scribbling of an old woman who had only recently emerged from illiteracy. I still didn't know which one among the six boarders the man had been. He seemed to be amused by my question and smiled knowingly, pulling up the collar of his black coat.

"Who else but 'the business student who had only one outfit per season'. Wasn't that what K used to call me?"

Saying his goodbyes, the man stood from his chair and walked swiftly toward the exit, leaving without hesitating. Just like that, his black coattails vanished from sight. I lifted my teacup and slowly brought it to my lips. The cup had completely cooled, with a single drop of tea pooled at the bottom, which trickled down and came to a stop halfway to my lips. After the man had gone, I stayed at the teahouse a while longer. When I finally settled my check and headed outside, my body felt curiously lighter.

2

AROUND THE END of March, a motorcycle messenger from a courier service delivered an envelope to my dorm. It contained a map and a bunch of keys on a ring. I peered inside the envelope and shook it out, but nothing else was inside. There wasn't any handwritten note explaining how J, after remembering how much his mother had trusted me, decided to put me in charge of the inn or how to take care of the bills and taxes. There was no memo assuring me that at least the heat and electricity were on or that I could stay there until the end of spring. I didn't even have a number to call in case of an emergency. Only my name was written on the outside of the envelope, and I recognized the crude handwriting at once. The address of the inn was written in the same hand at the top of the map.

W was a small city located in the mountainous eastern region of the country. When I was about to slide the map back inside the envelope, I saw that its bottom corner had worn away and was on the verge of tearing. It had probably rubbed against the keys. That reminded me of W: During a trip a while back, I'd stopped at a museum dedicated entirely to old prints. An ancient map displayed on the wall had a small hole around its center. A map is something that you fold up and carry around, the guide had explained. The hole forms there, because the very center of the map gets the most wear and tear. The hole was W. "So does that mean the hole is the center and also the starting point?" I recalled S asking. It was our last trip together before S and I broke up. The term "starting point" got my attention and I gazed at the old map, which I'd had absolutely no interest in at first.

The center that had been swallowed by a black hole because it had worn away after being folded up and stowed away for so long—that place was W.

A few days later, I went to a bookstore looking for a map of W. The map I found was of very poor quality.

"Is this all you have?"

"That's all we've got."

Fortunately, the bookstore clerk knew a place where they sold more detailed maps. It was a small specialty bookstore located on a side street in the center of town. But getting there was not as easy as his hasty directions had made it out to be. Only after walking up and down along the same path a number of times did I discover it across the street near the corner. It was in a quiet neighborhood without much traffic, but I backtracked to find a crosswalk anyway. I remembered something S had said. "You're so square. Don't you know the rules of the real world are messed up to begin with? Do you think you can bring order to this world by following all of them to a tee?" Would she be in some church right now, praying she be allowed to keep a closer eye on me even after leaving me?

The owner of the bookstore, a man in reading glasses, greeted me from behind the counter. Blocking my line of sight was a bookshelf made out of a bunch of little rectangular compartments stuffed with countless rolled-up maps of various sizes. When I told him I was looking for a map of W, he asked me whether I preferred English, Chinese characters or Korean.

"Korean, please."

Before I finished speaking, a map was already on the counter, rolled into a scroll, as though the man had just pressed a button on a vending machine. I unrolled the map slowly, and for whatever reason, the college campus was the first thing I saw. Maybe because it was the satellite campus of my alma mater, or it could be that it was right by a lake. When looking at a map, one is bound to notice the mountains and the bodies of water first.

When I checked the address, J's inn wasn't very far from

campus. The college was located where the lake ended, and approximately four kilometers beyond the campus was the beginning of a steep mountain pass. From either side of the pass, there were trails going up the mountain. The inn was located at the trailhead—a good spot for hikers who wanted to climb up the mountain the next morning and needed a place to stay for the night. It seemed likely that there would be a restaurant nearby as well.

The owner of the bookstore took my money and spoke as he removed his reading glasses.

"It's probably still cold up there. The ground is heavy with moisture and the valleys run deep. It's a terrain surrounded by vile energy."

"Is there much wind?"

"How could there not be, at the crest of the pass."

Only after leaving the bookstore did I start wondering how the owner had known that my destination was at the peak of the mountain pass, but I forgot all about it while re-crossing the street. My body somehow seemed to be getting lighter and lighter.

3

THE GAS STATION and the restaurant were in a secluded spot a long way from town. From there began the steep pass, at the crest of which stood J's forlorn three-story inn. As I'd expected, the paint job on the inn's sign had all but worn away, the windows all securely shut and the outer walls dirty, giving off a gloomy, almost eerie air. It was late afternoon by the time I parked my clunker of a car in the vacant back lot. The shadows from the forest hung over everything so that it was already getting dark.

I tried a bunch of keys until I found the one for the front door and opened it. As soon as I set foot in the empty building, the distinct odor of mold and disinfectant that all such inns seem to carry invaded my nostrils. The interior looked cleaner and brighter than what I expected, based on the way things had looked on the outside. The first floor held the innkeeper's living quarters, the kitchen, and other functional facilities like the storage room. The guest rooms were located on the second and third floors. I walked up to the second floor carrying my bags and stood for a while in the middle of the hallway to pick out a room. I went past the first room and entered the second room. It was Room 203. When I opened the window, I could see the bottom of the hill directly below. The serpentine road wound all the way down the steep slope. The lake and the college campus were visible in the distance, framed by the mountains.

Inside, the room was exactly as I'd imagined. Two pillows were laid out on the bed, and installed on the small table next to it were a tiny water cooler and cups. The room had a mirror, a plain old dresser with a comb, a hair dryer, and bottles of lotion.

The linoleum floor had a few cigarette burns, and the wall had nothing but two wire hangers dangling on nails. I took off my jacket and hung it on one of the hangers. I couldn't think of anything to do, so I flopped down on my back on top of the covers. With my arms crossed under my head, I stared vacantly for a long time at the jacket on the hanger. I thought back to the man in the black coat's younger self.

Back then the boarders had established a routine of playing round after round of *hwatu* every night. Except for the handsome engineering student who was never around and the older of the two medical students, the remaining four became regulars: the younger medical student, the whiny law student, the business student with just one outfit per season, and the English student who was good with a guitar. They almost always played in my room. They'd enter my room en masse, while offering up some excuse about my room being the cleanest or that, since I was the housemother's favorite, it wouldn't look as bad if they gambled in my room. I'd sit at the desk with my back to the cards, but eventually I'd get sucked in by the rowdiness of the game and end up watching. The law student was always the first to start winning money. But as time passed, the medical student and the English student would expand their powers little by little so that when the clock was about to strike midnight, there wouldn't be much of a difference in how much any of them had won or lost. Around then, the older medical student would come through the door with his first warning for his brother, telling him to give it a rest. There would be one or two more warnings after that. Every time the medical student heard the wind blowing from the Windy Mountain, he'd think it was his older brother coming up the stairs and scurry under my blanket and pretend to be sleeping. He'd do this over and over again, but he wouldn't stop playing cards.

The law student's face would grow anxious and contorted each time he lost a hand, and the moment he got a fresh start by recouping his principal sum, his eyes would get all veiny and red.

His impatience caused him to make more than a few mistakes. The help I patiently offered him from the sidelines was of absolutely no use to him. The English student appeared relaxed and free when he played, probably because he had plenty of money. He racked up points little by little so that it was barely noticeable, then when the decisive moment came he would invariably crush the law student. Without a doubt, he enjoyed not only playing the game but manipulating the law student's mood, too.

By dawn, everyone's concentration had dipped and nerves were frayed. Words became few and far between, and you could feel the tension—the sound of each card cutting through the silence. It was the business student with the single outfit per season who would play best at this time and suddenly sweep the whole pot. He always played *hwatu* while wearing his suit jacket. The sight of his profile as he sat upright in his suit jacket until the break of dawn was chilling, like that of the grim reaper. Everyone was eager for the game to end soon, but nobody seemed capable of much else but blinking and mechanically dealing out the cards, each imprisoned in his powerlessness. The business student wore the same jacket spring, fall and summer but in winter he wore a coat—again, his only one—over the jacket. He'd smile knowingly at me when I asked him if he ever thought about buying himself some new clothes with the money he won playing. He'd laugh and tell me that buying more clothes only led to more laundry.

Now that I think about it, I'd heard the man laugh like that once before. The vague image of him wearing his black coat again and leaning against the prow came to me. I'd been sitting beside him while gazing down at the river flowing below. The man turned his head toward me and fixed his eyes on something behind me. Then he made that knowing smile. It was cold so the breath came out in white puffs. I wondered what had been behind me that had made him smile that way.

Realizing that the room had gone completely dark, I got up from the bed.

4

THIS NEIGHBORHOOD WAS in the outskirts of town, too desolate to call a university district per se. There were clusters of studio apartment buildings, tiny convenience stores, pool halls and restaurants and not much else. Just a few steps beyond these a dark field, a vacant lot, and farmhouses with some scattered lights appeared. There weren't many people walking down the street, either. When I caught a glimpse of a bar around the corner, I made up my mind to have a beer instead of dinner and stopped the car. It was an underground bar in a small two-story building that housed a real estate office on the first floor. The sign was lit, but even before I set foot down the darkened stairway, I could feel that the place gave off a chilly, foreboding air. When I made the turn at the landing, I saw someone crouching at the foot of the stairs.

I stopped in my tracks. The person must have heard my footsteps because their head turned in my direction. It was a young woman with long wavy hair.

"It must've closed because of exams. Nobody ever comes here except students."

The woman introduced herself as a student who worked part-time at the bar.

"The owner doesn't call to let me know he's not opening. This is the second time already."

The woman's demeanor made me somewhat uncomfortable—talking to a complete stranger, and a man at that, without appearing to be guarded or nervous at all. After nodding my head slightly, I started to retreat up the steps. From behind me, her voice sounded friendly.

"Wait. I'll show you another place where you can get a drink."

The woman was already getting up as she spoke.

At first, I thought that the woman, in the process of standing up, had decided to sit back down. True, she was several stairs below me, but still she appeared astoundingly short. Showing no interest in my reaction, she went up the stairs past me, treating me genially as though she were some kind of guide. It was then that I realized she was a dwarf, with short arms and legs and a chubby build. Her hair was tied with a ribbon fashioned out of a strip of fabric. She wore a flared dress with a frilled hem and red platform shoes about the length of my hand. I stood there for a moment, dumbfounded. The woman turned around to face me.

"It's not far. I'll pay for the drinks if you want."

I imagined her paying the tab with a gypsy bracelet, or with silver coins she'd take from a bundle belonging to a circus troupe.

There weren't many customers at the bar as I'd expected. The draft beer wasn't very good, but it was so cold that it went down easy before I could really taste it.

The woman knew about J's inn. When I told her that I'd be staying there for the time being, she looked at me intently.

"I can sleep there tonight, right?"

She made very little effort to keep others at a distance, let alone to guard herself against men she didn't know. While swallowing a mouthful of beer, I tried to formulate an appropriate response.

"The building's been abandoned for some time, and it's way out in the middle of nowhere. It's kind of creepy. You'd be okay with that?"

"I've already been there many times before."

The woman said this as if it were nothing. For some reason I couldn't bring myself to probe for details. Though I wasn't sure what or why, I had the feeling I might end up hearing something sinister.

"Would you mind if I used a couple different rooms?"

When I asked if she had friends she wanted to bring along, she shook her head.

"Ever since I was little I wanted to live in a house with lots of rooms. I'm talking about one of those houses you see where all the rooms are brightly lit. My house didn't have very many rooms but still my mother always told me to turn off the lights every time I left the room. When I was little, I thought turning off the lights would frighten the people who were still in the room."

"Who was still in the room?"

"That's the thing. As a child, I had a pretty wild imagination. Even when I was by myself, I thought there was always someone in the room with me. I probably didn't like the idea of being by myself in a room. My mother always told me to shut the door behind me, but of course I never listened. I was stubborn and said it would be rude if I shut the door behind me when there were still people on their way out. Don't other children pretend like this?"

I'd only pictured things exactly as they'd been described in books. Your nose would grow if you told a lie, for instance, or a frog would leap out of your mouth every time you tried to speak if you didn't give a beggar change.

"I even imagined I could float around in midair. I really believed that if I could just make my body light enough I would be able to float in the air."

"Really? How do you make yourself so light?"

"I had to split up into many me's. I thought it would help to have many rooms. When I was a kid I thought I wasn't getting taller because my height had to be divided up between all the different me's."

"Do you still think that?"

"No, I'm not a kid any more. But this one time something quite strange did happen.

"I was working at a ticket booth in an underground parking garage at the center of the city. It was one of those areas with towering buildings back-to-back, eight-lane roads jam-packed with cars honking their horns nonstop and shooting fumes from their mufflers. A part of the city where people bumped shoulders as they ran to the bus station, and the trees lining the streets were dying from those Christmas lights coiled tightly around the length of their trunks. But it was a whole other world when you came down into the garage—a place immersed in dark and dingy silence, where dozens of cars stretched out in rows, lying prostrate without a sound. The sight of the cars crowded together, with each car's arrogant, mean eyes seeming to keep the next car in check, reminded me of corpses awaiting their turn to be cremated. All around them were dark gray walls and partitions, the ordered numbers painted in black, not to mention the stillness and the cold that somehow sent chills deep into your body, whispering for you to make a run for it. The dank smell of cement particular to basements would mix with the smells of gasoline and automobile fluids, so that your breathing became labored the moment you entered. I was the one sitting there all day in that cramped booth by the entrance, staring vacantly at the gate, waiting for cars to arrive, like some broken doll someone had shoved through the booth's glass door and forgotten about.

"I worked in the oldest and most forlorn building in that district. Water would drip down on rainy days from the low cement ceiling with exposed the pipes. It felt like cold water was leaking from my entire body all day long while I sat in the tiny booth of that miserable parking lot, where all I had for company were cars lying in neat lines, like corpses. It was on one of those days that a black car rolled in, glimmering from the rain. Catching a glimpse of me out of the corner of his eye, the driver steered toward me instead of proceeding down the ramp to park. I made an effort to put on a polite smile, but that only seemed to upset the man further. 'That's odd,' the man said brusquely, the whites of his wide eyes popping out. 'Didn't I see you at a flower shop outside the city just now? You were getting soaked in the rain without an umbrella, weren't you? I definitely saw you bringing the flower pots back inside—so how can it be that you're sitting here?'

"Something similar happened not long after that. A coworker who had come to relieve me was all worked up. 'She was sure it was you! The woman who works the booth on the first floor just came from the hospital, and she said she definitely saw you. She said she was surprised to see you being wheeled into the operating room. You know how you stick out. It would be hard to mistake you for someone else.' 'Where could I possibly go while I'm on my shift? Besides, I've never been sick enough to be hospitalized.' When I told her this, my coworker laughed, 'What are you saying, there's more than one of you?' She added, 'Is it because all dwarves look the same?' I got fired about a month later. Quite a few people must have told the manager that the sight of a dwarf sitting completely still in a booth is just too disturbing.

"That's when I found myself daydreaming again. Let me explain.

"There are several me's spread out all over the world, living in different places and at different times. They're all very different. There's a me who gets angry easily, a me who is very shy, a me who is a very good with words, a me who is foolish. There's a me who is beautiful and a me who is hideous. They all exist separately, but if at one point they all think the same thought, we suddenly become apparent to other people. If all the me's feel lonely, for example, then I start hearing about them from people: 'I saw a vulgar you cursing up a storm in the market yesterday trying to haggle over the price.' 'I saw an elegant you at the opera, completely absorbed in the performance, crying up in the balcony.' 'I saw an old you in a greenhouse picking a cucumber, hunched over at the waist.' 'I saw a serene you wearing a wide-brimmed hat, reading a book on a park bench.' 'I saw a crazy you covered in blood and chasing after your man after he gave you a beating.'

"But people forget these incidents soon enough. Lots of people in this world look alike, and people believe that it's absolutely impossible for one person to appear in several places at once."

"So are you saying this isn't just you daydreaming?"

"Yes, everything I've just told you is part of my daydream. If you let me use many rooms, I think I'll be able to settle each of my many selves in a room of her own and fall asleep feeling very light."

"This is absurd."

"Because it's a daydream. Since that incident, I've wondered from time to time if the childhood game of dividing yourself up into many selves ever stops."

After finishing her long story, the woman lowered her eyes and raised the mug of beer slowly to her lips.

She'd gone to the trouble of applying makeup, as if to prove she was an adult, but it made her face look very unnatural, as though someone had painted heavy makeup on a doll. Her reddened cheeks would have hid her deep-set eyes were it not for their unusual sparkle. She seemed stronger than she looked, judging by how easily she lifted the mug full of beer between her first finger and thumb, so short and chubby, like a child's.

"People often think dwarves have a special talent. Because of the defect in our physique, they think we exist in a realm beyond the rules of the physical world. But we just haven't grown, that's all. Nobody else was born with my condition in our family, except for my first cousin."

The woman said that W was her hometown, but even before she'd turned twenty years old she'd begun to wander from place to place. She'd already helped out at an inn run by a relative in a university district in Seoul, and she'd enrolled in quite a few training programs, trying to learn one skill or another. She'd held a variety of part-time jobs, all of which entailed answering phones or working the register.

"There was nothing I was particularly good at. It wouldn't take long for me to get fired."

"I had one employer but they fired me six months later."

She gently pressed the back of my hand with her palm, as if in consolation; it was a friendliness offered beyond what I'd expected. She went on.

"If there's anything I am good at . . . It's not climbing ropes or tricks like that. It's strange, but when I talk to someone for a long time, it seems like I start reading the other person's mind a little. When you came to W, was it to meet somebody?"

I told her no.

"I guess you could say I was trying to get out of a rut. Like when you go on a trip. Have you by any chance heard of the temple you get to by boat? It's near this city. I was thinking of going there tomorrow."

When I asked her if she'd come along, she nodded. I felt an odd sense of relief and then began to tell stories from a long time ago as they came to me.

"I went there one winter. It was fifteen years ago. There were seven of us, and we were all cheerful from the moment we set off for the trip. The winds over the river were fierce but we were drinking on the boat, so everyone was in a good mood."

This was around the time that the housemother was running the small inn down the alley. At the start of winter vacation, the boarders, having gone their separate ways, had decided to pay her a visit. All seven boarders showed up and sat together in the inn's living room. It was dark, with only a single window no bigger than the palm of your hand in the hallway, and the air was musty with a heavy, indistinct odor. Everyone else had found rooms in other boarding houses except for the business student with only one outfit per season, who was sharing a room with J there at the housemother's inn. He was telling a story that day about a job interview he'd had. He'd accidentally burned a hole in the sleeve while ironing his one and only suit jacket, and ended up going to the interview with his jacket sleeves rolled up. The interviewers had asked him if he often sweated excessively, and kindly encouraged him to relax. In the end it turned out that among the six of them who were about to graduate later that year, he was the only one who had secured a job. When one of them said he always thought that I'd be the first one hired, everyone except for me, for some reason, burst out laughing. Another guy added that the two of us had gone to the same school the same year and majored in the same subject, and wasn't my GPA higher than his? The laughter wouldn't stop even when the housemother entered the room, carrying a serving tray with both hands. I said the business student could now throw out his ratty clothes and get a new outfit with the arrival of every new season, but my words were completely drowned out by their laughter.

There wasn't any fruit or tea on the housemother's serving tray but an assortment of items like wrist watches, student IDs, and rings. I saw buttons, hairpins, even a necklace that someone must have taken off and then forgotten about. "See if anything catches your eye." She added that they were nothing fancy, just items that guests hadn't remembered to pick up after leaving them in deposit for a night's stay at the inn, sounding as if she were apologizing for insufficient hospitality on her part. One of the boarders made a joke by saying, "Hey, maybe I know one of these guys," as he fished through the different ID cards on the tray before yelling out, "Hey K! This guy has your name! Your year of birth is the same too. Hey, maybe you're one of those deadbeats who ran off without paying!" The housemother put an end to the matter by saying she'd never have given anyone a room with just an ID card as collateral. One of them jokingly suggested that when they went to take the boat to the temple, they should each carry one of these strangers' IDs with them, just for fun. They were all laughing, each trying to pick out the stranger's ID with the name and age closest to his own. I was the only one who hadn't known in advance about this trip.

That's when I began to wonder, how long have things been this way? How long had things been going on right under my nose, without my noticing? And since when had I been excluded from their circle?

"So you got on the boat with those IDs?"

"Yes."

"Why?"

"I don't know. I just wanted to throw it from the boat. I wanted to pretend I was throwing myself into the river. I think I was getting a little tired of myself."

"But it was someone else's ID."

"You're right. But when I saw the ID drifting away in the water, my body felt strangely lighter."

The woman looked at the wall behind me, her face void of expression.

"And right after that, I think, I jumped into the river."

The sparkle in her eyes, as she held my gaze, rippled gently under the lights, like water in a pool.

"Everyone on the boat must have thought I jumped in after the ID because I accidentally dropped it in the water. Everyone else was sitting along the opposite side of the boat looking down-river and only the business student, wearing his black coat over his jacket, to my right. I looked back at him because he called my name. The business student put on that knowing smile of his. That very moment, I leapt into the water. As if on cue."

"Why don't we order some more beer?"

Her tone of voice was tender, as if trying to console a child. I was covered in cold sweat for some reason. I spoke in a hurried voice, as if I were running away from something.

"Okay. Now why don't you tell me more about yourself. You know . . . who did you used to have a crush on, things like that."

A smile lit up her face.

"There was this guy who used to call me Gelsomina. He told me that she was a character in a movie. The dwarf wife of a gypsy strongman. This guy played the guitar for a living. He'd show up carrying his bulky guitar case at a restaurant where I used to work part-time. He'd come in late at night and order coffee, telling me that anytime a tired-looking man carrying an instrument came by for coffee late at night I should make the coffee especially strong and hot, because the man was probably a poor, talentless wage slave who was about to be fired any day now. It would be even better if I gave him my prettiest and purest smile, since there was no greater consolation in this world than the presence of a kind, warm-hearted woman. I'd sit across from him and tell him stories, the way I'm telling you now. I'd let him know that the reason I never grew very tall was because I'd been divvied up into multiple selves. I'd tell him I wouldn't be lonely because there were so many of me in this world—that loneliness might mean longing for one of my other selves. I always paid for the man's coffee. It's strange. I have a soft spot for people who need something from me. I don't know whether he listened to my stories, but, at the end, he'd always say the same thing: 'You really look like sad little Gelsomina. That makes me Zampano, the violent man who lashes out at you with an iron chain. I was beating you last night in my dreams. I'm sorry.' He would bury his face in my shoulder and mutter, while sobbing to himself, 'I'm sorry. I'm a useless bastard.' After awhile, the guitar player didn't come in for coffee anymore. Maybe he did finally get fired."

"I don't know, people tend to get sadistic toward those who are submissive. If someone treats you kindly, sometimes you want to stomp all over them. Like when you know full well what the other person wants to hear, but it's the last thing you want to give in and say."

Her eyes opened wide, as if she had no idea what I was talking about. I emptied my beer mug in one gulp. I was swaying back and forth; the scene before my eyes was losing focus.

"Did you ever hear him play the guitar?"

"Yes, after closing time. He told me that this song was about how all human beings are strangers to each other."

People are strange when you're a stranger.
Faces look ugly when you're alone.
Women seem wicked when you're unwanted.
Streets are uneven when you're down.
No one remembers your name.
When you're strange. When you're strange.

"One of my cousins loved that song, so I know it well."

"The cousin who's short like you?"

"He was doing business in the city, but then he quit and returned to his hometown. Now he's running a roadside restaurant near a gas station."

It occurred to me that it must be the restaurant at the foot of the steep slope leading up to J's inn.

"The truth is, he was in prison. He was sent away several times, after getting expelled from middle school. He lived in a university district around that time and he said he learned the song from some college student."

"Why did he get expelled?"

"He was sniffing industrial glue with his friends in a deserted lot at the end of an alley and caused a fire somehow. The police were able to track down witnesses, so the school found out about it. He could no longer stay in town."

"Do you by any chance know a tall man who always goes around in a black coat?"

She shook her head, her eyes wide.

I let out a long yawn. I suddenly felt as if I couldn't keep my eyes open much longer.

"The two of us used to live in the same house a long time ago. I ran into him at a teahouse, and he mailed me some keys. That's how I ended up going out to buy a map of W. While I was looking for a crosswalk, I remembered something my girlfriend always used to tell me; that I'd staked my whole life on the belief that I'm the only one who's right, that I didn't have a clue about the world."

"What does that mean?"

"I have no idea."

My eyes were growing so heavy, I could barely answer her.

5

I COULDN'T SLEEP well, with the windows rattling all night. The wind sounded like the lashing of a whip, mixed with the sounds of crying, and all of the sudden, I thought I could hear footsteps. That's probably why I had a dream of being dragged away and beaten by a gang. After waking from the nightmare, I stayed still for a long time and looked up at the ceiling, at first confused about where I was. My whole body was soaked in sweat. It wasn't the strangeness of the position of my body, the smells that surrounded it, the texture of the bedding, the stuffy air, or the stillness that felt like being underwater. I felt powerless with despair. It demanded that I surrender to the fatigue and made me so immobile I couldn't even lift a finger.

I was thirty-five years old when I got my first job. I was hired as the assistant to the head of a law firm. All that I had left at the end of my short career was a used car I couldn't pay to give away and the verdict of the general public that I couldn't cut it in the modern work environment. When S learned that I'd left the firm, she teared up. "How can you be so self-centered," she said, piling on one more judgment against me. Until then, I'd never thought deeply about how I was perceived by others. I'd always treated the question "Who am I?" as nothing more than a prompt on a personality test, amusing at best, and dismissed it as an idle thought fit for adolescents. I was pained by the sight of S's tears, but not because I felt like I'd disappointed her. It was my realization that who I am matters less than how I'm perceived—that there was no way of getting beyond that characterization once people made up their minds. It was around then that my nightmares became more frequent.

The woman was still sleeping. I could hear her faint, regular breaths, so in sync with my own heartbeat that it sounded as though the two might harmonize to form a chord. I couldn't remember exactly how I'd gotten back to J's inn the night before. I remembered the woman going up and down the stairs in a flurry of activity, getting the old inn back in operation. She turned on the heating system, tested the toilets, checked for hot water, hunted down a flashlight and some other tools, and fetched fresh supplies like towels and toilet paper. Like some kind of an errand fairy who had developed the ability to divide herself into many selves, she went back and forth, up and down, completing several tasks at once. She had the remarkable ability to search out a role for herself, regardless of situation, and win recognition for being useful. At the same time she had a sense of slightness about her, making it easy for people to take her for granted. Even if her multiple selves came together, she'd still not achieve full height.

It occurred to me that I might have seen her splitting into many different selves the night before while I was drunk. I recalled seeing two dwarves sitting across from me at one point. I thought this was what one of them had said: "It's been a long time. I didn't mean anything by it. When I heard that he'd run into K by coincidence, I just really wanted to meet up with him. I was curious about how he was doing."

I waited for dawn to break and went out to the backyard where I saw my car parked all by itself, splattered with dirt leaves, as if it had been rolling around in mud. I couldn't see very clearly—the sky, the woods, and the air itself were all tinged by reddish fog. Yellow dust from China had descended upon us.

The woman came up behind me. "Did I drive last night?"

"My cousin did. Not many places to drink around here. So I guess you guys know each other? I heard you telling him you'd have breakfast at his restaurant."

I told her I didn't have any appetite at all.

6

IT WAS ALMOST noon when the woman and I pulled up at the dock. It was so completely deserted, it was hard to imagine a more desolate place. When we checked the ferry schedule, we found out it only made two trips a day. Having sensed the presence of people, an old woman thrust her head out the door of the corner store. "Not many people want to take the ferry anymore since the road for cars has been completed," she said brusquely, and clutched the door as if she was about to slam it shut.

"You can get there by car? I thought it was an island."

"An island? It's just a long way to travel on a mountain trail, so people used to get there by crossing the river."

"How long will it take to drive to the temple?"

The old woman stared straight at me.

"There's no temple. There's only the site of the temple."

"Was it torn down?"

"There was no temple there in the first place. No, maybe I heard one used to be there, until a few hundred years ago."

"But I saw the name of the temple printed on the map. I even saw a sign."

"Just because you see the name of the temple doesn't mean the temple is going to be there. Maybe the map forgot to indicate that it's just the ruins. And maps can be wrong. Mapmakers are only human."

"I guess I didn't think of that."

The old woman asked me whether I still wanted to buy a ticket. When I told her no, the door to the store swung closed behind her.

After getting in the car again, I told the woman we should head back. It occurred to me that my memory of sneaking into the temple's main hall in the dead of night, of lying on a wooden floor cold enough to send shivers through my bones, might have been of a different temple. Now it seemed I'd gone into the main hall by myself, and if that were the case, maybe the entire memory was wrong. But the woman said she wouldn't miss out on seeing the river after coming this far and stubbornly got out of the car. She brushed past me and led the way, once again like some amiable guide. Her steps were astonishingly quick. Both the ribbon tying her long, wavy hair and her flared skirt seemed to fly in the wind as I followed behind her reluctantly. Before I knew it she was already entering the path down through the pine groves along the river. The yellow dust that had followed us there was blurring everything. I saw the woman climb atop a tall, jutting rock and straddle it.

"I don't think I did any experiments on how to become lighter." I told her while trying to catch my breath. "It's just what I happened to be thinking when they pushed me into the river. I wished my body could become light. I wished that I could float up into the sky."

The boarders had all hated me and tortured me routinely with their mean-spirited pranks. The older of the two medical students never exchanged a word with me. Just once he came looking for me in my room and asked me whether his younger brother had really been sleeping or if he'd been playing cards, and I was incapable of lying. The *hwatu* rounds broke up after that. But card games aside, the whiny law student continued to borrow money from me. He knew I wouldn't play dumb and say I didn't have any money to lend him. He also knew that if he told me later he didn't have the money to pay me back, I wouldn't have the courage to call him out and say, "You're lying to me, aren't you?" It was the same case with the handsome engineering student. When he brought a girl home and wanted to hide her in my room, I couldn't make up some excuse to get out of it. And while I did see J and his friends from time to time, going down an alley late at night carrying a *soju* bottle and some glue wrapped in a plastic bag, I wasn't spying. It was merely a scene that anyone standing by the window would have naturally encountered.

When the English student who was good with a guitar learned that I liked Jim Morrison, he taped the word "DOORS" to my door.

"What does it mean?" I asked him.

"Isn't it just like you to call a door a door?"

But I knew very well about the line from an English poem posted over his desk: "There are things known, and things unknown: in between are the doors" (William Blake).

Red ribbon in her wavy hair, her dress wide and frilled, the woman watched the river and swung her legs like a child left alone on the tall rock. She kept crossing and re-crossing her short legs dangling in midair. It suddenly occurred to me that I might have hurt S. I might have hurt this woman too. I might have hurt my family—maybe the whole world. What had I done wrong?

"Are you crying?"

"Because of all the yellow dust. I might get an eye infection."

"Liar!"

The woman threw her head back and cackled gleefully.

"I fell into the water while carrying someone else's ID. I dried myself off at the *minbak* house near the temple."

"They're all lies."

That's when it happened. The woman's body, along with her laughter, floated up into the air. I grabbed the hem of her skirt and at that moment I felt my own body floating up with her. In a whirl of reddish yellow dust, I could see the river off in the distance, and all the passengers crowding the boat, the man in a black coat, and the image of K in his younger days with his hands stuffed in his pockets, looking down the river with a hesitant expression, puffs of white breath coming from his mouth. So this is how it's done, I muttered to myself. I have finally completed my research on how to make my body lighter.

7

It was S's birthday. I took her to Ruby Tuesday's.

"Really? Ruby Tuesday's of all places? I'm too old to sit here and blow out candles with a tiara on my head."

S was full of complaints, but it was the only restaurant near the dorm that served Western-style food. Here and there, children were being rowdy. A server appeared dressed like a girl from the Alps. After greeting us with a curtsy, she asked us if we wanted the non-smoking section. "Yes, and can you seat us in a quiet area?" S said in a voice full of restraint, after shooting daggers with her eyes at the rowdy children.

"This is the only quiet spot at the moment. Is this okay?" The server had guided us toward a booth by a window, way off in the corner of the restaurant. How could such a quiet table still be available? Relieved, I slid into the booth first, sitting on the inside with my back to the wall. The space between the table and the bench was too tight, so I pushed the table away from me a little. Then S tried to seat herself across from me. But the opening was too narrow so that her body wouldn't fit between the table and the bench. S peevishly shoved the table back in my direction and tried to squeeze herself in. Needless to say, the table was practically touching my chest, and S's angry face wasn't far away. We ended up leaving our seats in the reverse order we'd taken them, and were guided to a table right next to the rowdy children, our mood now even worse.

"What's the point of having a booth where customers can't even sit down?"

The server gave S a ready response. "Something wrong with

the design, I guess. But some customers occasionally do sit there."

S and I barely exchanged a word over our steak and beer. We'd been seeing each other for ten years by then, so it wasn't like there was much left to talk about. Secretly, we knew that the moment we opened our mouths, we might blurt out that the whole thing had gotten tedious or that we should just break up. That day, we drank late into the night. Most of the customers had left by then, so for the first time, the atmosphere was quiet, just like S had wanted. I saw a man being guided to the cramped booth where S and I had tried to sit. He was carrying a large instrument case, and there were streaks of gray in his hair. He looked tired. The waitress guiding the man was so short she might have been a dwarf. I didn't think it was such a strange sight, since this was a family restaurant known for hosting special events. After pouring some coffee for the man, the short waitress took a seat across from him and they started talking. The booth fit them perfectly. The man lowered his eyes and drank his coffee without a word. The woman laughed occasionally while looking off into space with googly eyes, talking to herself in an animated way. From where we were seated, she looked like a mime. Every time the woman moved, the instrument case leaning against the wall blocked some of the lighting, casting a broad shadow across her face. Soon, the man rose from his seat, and pushed the table aside to sit next to the waitress. As soon as he sat down, he leaned his head on the dwarf woman's shoulder. I stared blankly at the sight of this man, who was now sobbing.

S suddenly called out in a low voice. "That sign was on our left a while ago, but now it's on our right. I'm positive. I'm positive it was over there!"

Slowly I brought the beer mug to my lips and slurped up the foam as I spoke. "It's a revolving restaurant. It turns a few degrees every second, and once every hour it returns to the same position."

"What? You should have told me so from the start!" There were tears in S's eyes. "Everything you do is like this. I know you want to tell me it's not your fault that the place is a revolving restaurant. You always go by the principle that you're never wrong, so in the end, nobody's to blame. Right?"

S's voice must have been a bit loud because the musician and the dwarf woman seated across from us turned to look at us. That's when I knew that the woman's eyes had met mine. Under her flared skirt, her short, neatly tucked legs were dangling in midair. And that's when I felt a part of me split from myself, float up, and drift toward the musician. The me who had crossed over to sit beside the dwarf woman began sobbing, my face buried in her shoulder. "I'm sorry, I kept on muttering. I'm sorry. I'm a useless bastard. I'm sorry." It didn't seem like my tears would stop any time soon.

Translated by Jae Won Chung

WEATHER AND LIFE

B's Daydream

B THOUGHT THAT she'd astonish the world someday. She didn't know what it would be exactly; only that one day, something would suddenly happen. If her present state was all there was, her life was too tedious.

Perhaps she'd inherit a vast estate from some distant relative whose face she hadn't even seen, like Little Lord Fauntleroy. She frequently lost herself in daydreams. What if she happened to discover some ancient treasure, hundreds of years old, buried in the corner of the yard? Or if she were to help a scruffy vagabond child on his way, only to find out that he was hiding his real identity and was in fact the son of the president, tired of his magnificent surroundings, off in search of a true friend. And if the person in need of help wasn't a boy but an adult, he could be a movie director in search of a young actress who, though on the surface quite ordinary in appearance, possessed a unique, hidden charm.

B's imagination was her only friend on the tiresome trips home from school. One day, she stopped and stood for a long time in front of a poster advertising the performance of a world-renowned Korean soprano. It wasn't because such a high-level classical performance was a rare occurrence in the small town she lived in. Instead, she was thinking that the magnificent, beautiful female singer might have insisted on volunteering for a provincial tour in order to find her real daughter. B imagined herself following her real mother on tour around the world.

No one knew when or how such instantly life-changing events might occur. B was especially friendly toward strangers. Moreover, she had a tendency to accept common, trivial, everyday matters as signs of something more significant. To anyone else, it was ordinary to see a row of neatly-placed shoes in disarray, or have a neon sign light up in front of one's eyes, or hear church bells suddenly ring while walking down the street. But every time such a thing happened to B, she'd carefully look around, her attention focused. When she walked, she'd often glance behind as if someone was following her; all anyone would have to do is tap her on the shoulder, and she'd jump with fright. Graffiti was another thing that attracted her interest. It was just random scribbling to a normal person's eyes, but to B it could be a message from beyond sent to her alone.

B's imagination expanded the limits of her four-dimensional world. She'd always considered it necessary to exercise caution on one's path, particularly at forks in the road. Choosing which direction to follow can, after all, completely change one's life. Consequently, the moment she set foot in one direction, she'd close her eyes tightly in acceptance of the future consequences of her choice. But at some point she'd begun to think that there was an abundance of invisible boundary lines throughout the world. To unintentionally cross these lines meant to be sucked into a black hole and thrown into another dimension. People were unable to perceive them; clearly all those who'd gone missing had crossed those boundaries and had gone into another dimension. Even in B's neighborhood, there was a gentleman of whom nothing had been heard in years. No one knew that he'd at some place and time stumbled upon one of those boundaries. Since normal people wouldn't even realize it if it happened to them, B considered life to be a dangerous, and at the same time dramatic, thing. Naturally she was different than other people.

It was a day when class was held outside, on the mountain behind the school. In search of a place to eat her packed lunch by herself, B stopped on a small trail. A huge log was blocking the way. A tree trunk had snapped in a typhoon the previous season and lay where it had fallen. To B, however, the log blocking the path looked like a border dividing the present world from a different, unknown world. At last, she'd come upon a boundary. She could clearly sense the flow of a mysterious, concentrated energy in the area, dizzying like a whirlpool. She felt a momentary chill run down her spine. She thought that the moment she stepped over the log, she might be entering a completely different world; there seemed to be unknowable beings enveloping her, watching over her decision with bated breath.

Unable to overcome her tension and dizziness, B suddenly collapsed to the ground. Her classmates sent word to the teacher in charge who came and helped her up, and thus B was able, just barely, to return to the normal world. She was scolded for walking away from the grounds of her beloved school, the "School of Love."

From that day forward, B began to think that she might have been born with a rare disease, regardless of the fact that her mother, when she heard what had happened, thought it was just a mild case of anemia and nothing to worry about. It was once difficult for her to understand why she'd been born into such mediocrity. But perhaps, since she was an exceptional individual, provision had been made for her to be raised as a normal person for her own protection. Her mind was supplied with one particular fancy, that through her rare disease she became aware of herself as one born of nobility. Ah, with life being full of so many codes, it's a wonder how many riddles we have to solve along the way.

Moving

B CONSIDERED HERSELF a duck who would one day leave for her real parents and become the crowned swan that she was born to be, just like in *The Ugly Duckling*. She wasn't too concerned about what was going on with her family. In fact, she'd always thought that the members of her household didn't care much about her. A family should have a special, anxious attachment to each other, like in *Little Women*. B's idea of a family was hiding presents deep in the backs of drawers, or looking down tenderly at sleeping faces, or standing at the window for a long, long time to watch one's child walk to school. Parents should always immediately stop whatever they're doing to lend an ear to their children's troubles; one need only look at *Hansel and Gretel* to see that big brothers should accompany and watch over their little sisters, wherever they happen to go. In that sense, there wasn't a single person in her family who acted like family. On top of that, in terms of an inability to recognize her uniqueness, her teacher and classmates were no different. B thought that she received unfair treatment from her family. The intimacy she shared with them was in fact normal, but it was difficult for B to accept wholeheartedly.

Since last winter, some change had taken place at B's home. With her parents quarrelling more frequently, her father had been away since January. They said he'd gone on a long-term business trip. And one day in February, her mother said that she was moving the family to a big city so that her second-oldest brother could go on to high school. With no word from B's oldest brother, as usual, her mother had no choice but to do the packing for the move by herself. She gathered all of the things up and put them outside: her husband's prized collection of books, his bicycle, his clothes and shoes; and the guitar, the record player, the set of dumbbells, the motorcycle posters on the walls, and other stuff scattered around her oldest son's room. But they didn't take any of it with them. They moved with little more than half of their household goods.

B's mother had the most trouble deciding whether to keep or to throw out the complete collection of *World's Classics for Boys and Girls* that stood in numerical order in the bookcase in B's room. She thought that at B's age, they were too childish for her, and that spending too much time reading storybooks would make her indifferent to study and more prone to indulge in wild fantasies. With B now about to enter middle school, there was no reason to take along a bunch of storybooks for children. Nevertheless, probably thinking that it would be wasteful to throw them away, she filled two boxes with them in the end and loaded them onto the moving truck.

Sitting with her mother in the truck's passenger seat, B arrived in a city she was seeing for the first time in her life. The place where they unloaded their things was an old neighborhood atop a hill on the outskirts of the city. The house had only two rooms; the wardrobe went in first, into the main room, and then B's second-oldest brother's desk was put in the room opposite. After the moving truck left, her brother, who'd taken the bus alone, stepped in through the gate late in the afternoon. He grumbled that he'd thought he was going to die trying to find the place and was seemingly displeased with both the house and the fact that they'd moved. For some reason he seemed to be severely angry with his mother, too. He trampled on B's neatly lined up shoes, stomped violently on the wooden floor, and if that wasn't enough, he mercilessly kicked apart the boxes of *World's Classics for Boys and Girls* that were lying off to the side of the narrow room. B resolved that when she transformed her life into something more splendid, she'd summon her brother just so that the look of surprise on his face would be the very first thing she'd see.

That night B's mother tossed and turned, groaning in pain. From under her blanket, B heard the sound of the cold spring wind ferociously shaking the windows. It appeared that everything was going to be different in this strange city. There was no longer a single person around who'd known the formerly ordinary B. Starting a new grade in a new school, she could become a completely different person. She tried to sleep. Just in case she composed a great poem in her dreams, and became famous overnight as a genius middle-school-student poet when it was published, she kept a pencil and paper at her bedside.

A Visitor

CHILDREN ARE INTERESTED in transfer students. But there wasn't much about B, who was always alone and lost in thought, to attract their curiosity. After a week or two, she'd become an inconspicuous child, just like she'd been in her hometown. Most of the children who took the bus to school hung around in small groups, but B was still alone.

One Saturday, the girls were especially restless and disorderly during clean-up time. Though Saturday was something they looked forward to anyway, this time they were also going to a movie after school. At the sound of the bell indicating clean-up time, the children hurriedly put aprons over their school uniforms and tied kerchiefs around their heads. They chattered on endlessly like a flock of sparrows sitting on a straw mat eating grain, even while moving around to the areas they were each responsible for. The weekend clean-up invariably included washing the windows. Standing one to a pane, the children looked as if they were busier with their chatting than with their cleaning. At a certain moment, a slight disturbance passed through them, and they all at once looked at the same place as if they were performing a military drill. Outside the walls of the school, it meant nothing, but at a girls' school during school hours, the appearance of a young man couldn't help but attract gazing eyes.

The man was slowly passing by the girls with a blank look on his face. He was tall and thin. His smart jacket and the black bag he carried in his hand made him look like an office worker; and with his prominent forehead and cheekbones casting a dark shadow on his face, his expression was not clearly visible. All of the girls at the windows craned their necks, their eyes following him until he disappeared through the staff room doorway.

B was sweeping the floor, indifferent to such disturbances. Not long after the man had passed, one of the students cleaning the staff room ran over to the classroom and called B's name. The teacher in charge had instructed her to come and get B. B decided to take off her apron and kerchief, not caring that it was still clean-up time. Like most first-years, she looked like a small child in her oversized school uniform. But her hands were trembling slightly as she gave it a sharp tug to straighten it out. As she slowly followed the other student out of the classroom, B was fully aware of the eyes of her classmates focused on her.

The man, standing in the corridor to the staff room, stared intently at B as she approached. There was no feeling at all in his dark, sunken eyes. His manner was businesslike rather than calm. But B was impressed by his exquisite silhouette against the backlight, long and dark like the shadow of the mysterious benefactor in the novel *Daddy-Long-Legs*. The man took B by the shoulder and led her over to the window as if he had a very secretive matter to discuss. He was a bill collector.

"You have a collection of *World's Classics for Boys and Girls* at your house, don't you?"

The tall man bent slightly toward B as he spoke, blinking his eyes. He lowered his voice to a whisper so as not to be heard by anyone else. A group of curious students walked past the corridor, glancing sideways at the pair. A heavy silence descended upon the man and B as they waited momentarily for the girls to pass. After they'd gone, the man slowly unzipped his black bag and took out an installment card with a number of spaces on it crowded tightly together. As soon as he confirmed that B's name was written in the contracting party's space and that not a single one of the spaces for payments made had been filled in, he promptly slipped the card back into his black bag, moving his hands as precisely as a magician. Only then did B realize that the reason her mother had kept those books was because not a single payment had been made on them.

"I don't want to humiliate you here at school."

Now extremely nervous, B stared up at the man's face, awaiting his next words.

"Are there any adults at your home?"

"My house is quite far away."

B wasn't unkind to strangers. But by the sound of her wavering voice, one could guess how much she wanted to avoid this situation.

"It doesn't matter whether it's far away."

The man's gaze was as cold as his response was predictable.

B bit her lip. Leading the bill collector to her home would be a betrayal of her family and land them in trouble. Her mother might not be her real mother, but B couldn't forsake the woman who was raising her. In fact, it was B's sincerity that kept the unfair treatment she received from her family from being unbearable. Her mother would be at a loss when B and the man walked through the gate, but surely she'd soon afterward give her daughter a sharp, questioning look. Her brother would thoroughly scorn her as thoughtless and disloyal, saying that he'd known all along she'd one day cause this kind of big problem.

"You can go to my house, but my father isn't there. Neither is my eldest brother."

B spoke the truth, but the man looked down at her with eyes that knew well enough the guiles of children.

"Is your mother not home either?"

At the man's incisive question, B's face reddened as if she'd been caught doing something bad.

The man kept watch on the entrance while B went back to the classroom to pack her schoolbag. He quickly recognized her coming out of the classroom in a gap among the other children, approaching him slowly, as if the air was pressing down on her. Holding his black bag at his side, he started to follow behind B as closely as her shadow. B's body stiffened as a chill ran down her back. It felt like several needles were poking into the back of her head, and she didn't seem to be able to breathe as deeply as she wanted. How many times in her life had she imagined that someone was following her? But even then, the person following her was always a dignified servant in search of his master's heir, or a genius film director, able to recognize her allure at first sight. Nowhere in B's broad and colorful imagination did the possibility exist that she'd one day suddenly become a criminal under strict observation, driven to a place she had no desire at all to go. To make matters worse, the moment B really wanted to avoid, that moment at the end of the laborious journey when they finally managed to reach her home, was waiting for her.

Around this time last year, B's mother decided to buy the complete collection of *World's Classics for Boys and Girls*. At first, she hadn't intended to buy any more storybook collections. The salesperson had recommended instead a complete collection of literature for young adults. However, it comprised thirty volumes, whereas the collection of *World's Classics for Boys and Girls*, with no less than fifty volumes, was the same price. Above all, it could be purchased under a special installment plan, where no payments had to be made for the first six months. Her mother especially liked those conditions. She'd found it strange, of course, that the bill collector never came, but she wasn't the kind of person to take the initiative to contact him first. Nevertheless, thought B, if he'd only come on the date when the payment was due, this kind of thing wouldn't have happened.

However B thought about it, she'd done nothing wrong. Above all, that she could be considered a bad person through no fault of her own made B feel mistreated and embarrassed. What's more, there didn't appear to be any hope that her innocence would be brought to light. The man didn't care if she was innocent or not, and being right or wrong in achieving his purpose didn't seem to be important to him, either. Without this kind of detachment, people carrying out orders could make up their minds to do whatever they wanted. B became worried. In this world, being right or wrong might have been unimportant right from the beginning.

Bus Stop; Traveling Together

THE BUS STOP was noisy with the clamor of students going to the movie theater. Every time a bus stopped, a portion of the children would crowd on all at once, their calves and book bags bumping into each other. The other passengers felt an assault on their hearing as if, instead of a group of schoolgirls, dozens of loudspeakers malfunctioning in high pitches had been suddenly loaded on. Each bus departed uneasily, as if about to burst, owing more to the boisterous sound of the schoolgirls, it seemed, than the fact that it was filled to capacity. B watched the girls with envious eyes.

Not that long ago, B too had planned to be part of the crowd getting on the crammed buses to go see the movie. She was supposed to have eaten instant noodles or *ddeokbokki* at the snack shop in front of the movie theater and then leaned back in one of the seats in the dark theater, looking up at the screen. But her present predicament was far removed from such everyday pleasures. B felt a burning sensation on the ridge of her nose. Her only desire was to go back to a time before the man had appeared. If her request could be granted, like in the story *The Three Wishes*, she wanted things the way they used to be. Also, B thought, time might be passing toward me from two different directions. It's moving in the present direction because I crossed one of the invisible boundary lines. Of all the lines on earth, I wonder how I happened to cross this line, the one that led this man, this bearer of bad news, to me.

"How did you find me?" asked B.

"They tell you who's assigned to which school at the education office."

Contrary to B's notion that her existence was completely hidden, it was apparently short and easy work to find a transfer student. The man informed her of one more fact.

"There are many ways to find out where someone has moved. But a reliable way of collecting debts is to go to the school first and let the children lead you to their homes."

The fact that the bill collector went to schools meant that he could find children and demand payment whenever he wanted. The parents had no choice but to pay. B didn't even want to think about the possibility of the man coming back to her school. She had no choice but to lead him to her home now. The Little Mermaid had only one way to return to the sea: to stab her beloved prince with a knife. It was the same for B. All she had to do to free herself from the man's watchful eye was lead him promptly to her mother. The Little Mermaid threw away the knife and became sea foam of her own free will, but for B there was no other option.

"Don't you take the bus?" asked the man when B walked past the bus stop.

"The bus doesn't go to our house." The words she'd prepared just a moment earlier sprung from her mouth awkwardly but quickly.

It was the first time she'd walked home from school, but if she kept following the string of bus stops, she had no fear of getting lost. Even though it was a few hours walk to her home, she wanted to make it more difficult for him. Against the man's authority as an adult and his absolute authority as a righteous executor, the only power B held over an older person like him was to bring him discomfort. As an extraordinary being, B couldn't behave obediently like a normal child.

Unskilled in the act of deceiving adults, B was surprised when she realized that she'd unknowingly quickened her pace and had to suddenly slow down. She looked back out of the corner of her eye and saw the man following quietly. Even so, her insistent heartbeat sounded urgent, as if it was about to jump out through the jacket of her school uniform. Acting as though nothing was wrong, she had to calm herself by secretly placing her hand over her heart. She let out a long sigh. She realized that if she was to be viewed as a bad person, she'd have to start doing bad things.

In Front of the Theater; Tears

B AND THE man walked down a road built along the embankment of a small stream. In the afternoon, the sunlight of the approaching spring was languid and warm. The light made gentle patterns in the water as it hit the shallow stream, and amid the verdant grass sprouting from the hills, there was an abundance of mugwort with its white inner leaves sticking out on display. On the branches of the cherry trees planted along the stream, the swollen flower buds seemed ready to burst any moment, the pink hue inside their light green coverings suffering from fatigue. The willow trees, like the rest, were busy absorbing the moisture under the hard soil through their wriggling roots, diligently pushing the fresh water up to their branches. It was a scene that B couldn't appreciate when she took the bus. A gentle breeze caressed her neck, which was exposed below her short bobbed hair.

Spring was everywhere. When they entered the street behind the theater, the abundance of lovers there, normal for a Saturday afternoon, caught their eyes. Some of them, lost in their own happiness, even smiled at the man and B as they approached, walking closely together. The students from B's school were nowhere to be seen. Those who'd taken the bus had arrived some time ago, and the movie they came to see had already started. None of B's classmates watching the movie would notice her absence. The small amount of attention that she'd received because of the special visitor would also have been forgotten.

A single teardrop sudden ran down B's face and dangled from the tip of her chin. Another tear fell from her face and made a spot on the toe of her running shoe. At first, she was at a loss. She'd wanted to maintain a dignified appearance right until the end of her encounter with the man, but she suddenly changed her mind. For fear that she should stop crying, she desperately started to think about sad stories: *Nobody's Boy*, about a boy who had to wander about all alone with a monkey as his friend; *3000 Leagues in Search of Mother*, in which a boy had to roam far and wide to find his mom, obviously; *A Little Princess*, about a girl who's treated cruelly, like a servant, by the arrogant and ugly Lavinia; *The Wild Swans*, the sad tale of a princess who, not allowed to speak under any circumstances, gets mistaken for a witch and is dragged off to be executed. Finally, B covered her face with both of her hands. Her book bag slipped from her grip and struck the sidewalk, her pencil case and books spilling out in a heap on the ground.

With her hands still on her face, she leaned against a telephone pole and sobbed. While one part of her was trying to think sad thoughts, her imagination was running wild. Passersby would approach B and ask her why she was crying, putting the man in an awkward situation. He couldn't tell them that he was leading her home in order to collect money. With any luck, a large gentleman would pass by and drive the man away, asking him why he was harassing a young girl. If it were her eldest brother, who never lost a fight, he'd definitely do that for her. B suddenly missed him, but he'd apparently crossed a boundary line to another dimension and gotten sucked into a black hole. Her father likewise wasn't a heartless brute who would simply pass by a crying child. Once he'd gotten off of his bicycle, he would, with his uniquely resolute expression, demand that the man explain himself. B moved her shoulders up and down with more and more intensity. Since the man may not have been aware of the anguish he'd inflicted upon a young child, it was necessary at that precise moment to make him ever more conscious of his wrongdoing. B was even prepared to faint, if necessary, as she had during her outdoor lesson at school.

But as B presently held her face in her hands, leaning against the telephone pole, there was no one around her. All the people were either going their own way or lingering in front of the theater. Those who couldn't get tickets because of the throng of students were busy talking among themselves about their plans for the day. No one was concerned about B. With his own black bag under his arm, and holding B's school bag in one hand and a cigarette in the other, the man simply waited with a blank expression on his face. He stuck out his lower lip and blew the cigarette smoke upward. He didn't even have the tolerance to wait for the persistent child to calm down. When he viewed a crying person, he looked as if he'd never experienced basic human sympathy. The man extended the school bag toward B, who, in order to put an end to her intense sobbing in the most natural way, sniffled intermittently while gradually slowing the movement of her shoulders.

"Isn't there a snack shop or something around here?"

He spoke calmly, as if he hadn't even seen B crying. Occupied as he'd been with riding the suburban bus since morning, he hadn't managed to eat a proper meal. B, having walked for so long that her legs hurt, and even having resorted to tears, was hungry, too.

Snack Restaurant; Delicious Ddeokbokki

THE MAN HAD asked for a plate of dumplings for himself and *ddeokbokki* for B. When B's stomach was full, her mind was much more at ease. The predicament of Jean Valjean, the poor, emaciated soul who stole a loaf of bread after going without food for three days, occurred to her. Seeing the man closely across the narrow snack shop table, he didn't really look that calm after all. When a dumpling slipped from his chopsticks and fell into the saucer of soy sauce, he reminded B of her impatient second-eldest brother as he clucked his tongue in frustration.

When they'd nearly finished eating, the man looked across at B and asked emotionlessly, "Does leading me to your home make you feel that victimized?"

As a sign of her agreement, B made no reply.

"They are your books, so it's your responsibility to pay for them."

"Even if I didn't purchase them?"

The man snorted derisively. "So you're telling me you've preserved the books like a treasure and haven't read a single volume?"

B felt a prick of conscience, but managed to find a reply at once. "I don't like the *World's Classics for Boys and Girls*. I've never even taken *The Iliad* or *Plutarch's Lives* or *Journey to the West* from the bookshelf. I don't know why people read difficult adventure stories like *Two Years' Vacation* and *Rasmus and the Vagabond*. I find absurd stories like *Cinderella* and *Snow White* really childish. And the stories with only unconditionally kind characters, how is that anything like the real world?"

"In any case, you have read the books, haven't you?"

The man placed a piece of *ddeokbokki* in his mouth and chewed it, making a sound as if he found it very tasty.

"I guess you don't like it, judging by the amount you've left uneaten."

Picking up the last piece with his chopsticks, he added, "So you don't intend to pay for it because it didn't taste very good, right?"

For just a moment, B felt a deep regret for having hoped to appeal to the man's sympathy with tears. How naïve she'd been to take solace, however fleetingly, in the possibility that he wasn't a bad person. But the man was simply making a joke, not illustrating the difference between right and wrong. Still, no matter which of the two he was doing, the result was the same. The man was as obstinate as an unmoving mountain; from the beginning, he was like a cold, haughty river flowing toward a fixed point. It wasn't easy to feel yourself being pulled along by its gentle current, but you still ended up arriving at a cliff. It was B's own problem, but there was nothing she could do by herself to change it. She was simply being carried off in the unrelenting flow. If there was anything that she could still do, it was to pray that the water changed course, that bad times would flow not toward her, but toward the man; in other words, the only thing to do was to desperately imagine that the man got trapped by an unknown boundary line.

As she was coming back from a trip to the washroom, B saw the man standing there, his keen eye keeping watch on the door to the ladies' washroom in the same way he'd watched her school's entrance. He had his eye on all doors. In that respect, there wasn't a single door open to B.

Stairs in the Alley; Escape

THE MAN WATCHED the street closely. He didn't walk right next to B, but he didn't let her get more than a few steps in front of him either. When B's pace changed even a little, he became aware of it immediately and adjusted himself to the new speed. Fast if she walked fast, slowly if she walked slowly, he wasn't caught off guard. When the bottom of a long staircase to her neighborhood came into view, B started to fret. She'd tried many times during their trip to her home to imagine a boundary line that would bring the man misfortune, but no sign of one appeared. A sewer manhole cover hadn't given way, nor had a hammer fallen from a construction site. He didn't twist his ankle or have his bag snatched or get bitten by a faithful dog, like the one in *Lassie Come-Home*. Nobody even asked him to become a prince for a single day, as in *The Prince and the Pauper*.

One more thing made B fretful. It was the anxiety she felt at the possibility that her mother didn't have any money. Of all the tragic scenarios that inevitably occurred to her every time she imagined what would happen when the man entered her home, this one was the worst. B started to consider the possibility that her family had become poor. Several things were different compared to when they were living in her hometown. Her mother looked weak many days and would lie down with a blanket wrapped around her, but she didn't go to the hospital. Maybe she didn't have any money to pay the hospital fee. It was possible, too, that a money problem was the reason her father and eldest brother were absent. B guessed that it was also the reason why her second eldest brother frequently told their mother in a sullen

93

voice that he wasn't planning to go to college.

As B's mind wandered with tragic visions of her family's poverty, it repeatedly arrived at her suspicion that her mother had
moved in order to avoid the bill collector. B bit her lip yet again.
Her mother, who had weakened considerably, might collapse
in a faint the moment she saw the man, even if it weren't true.
She'd manage to come to her senses, but she wouldn't recover
from the situation. She might grab the man by the collar and
tearfully beg him not to have her evicted from the house. B's
second eldest brother, sitting in his room silently mopping his
tears with his fists, would then use those same fists again to
strike the wall. B regretted her secret suspicion that her second
eldest brother was her mother's only real child. The poorer a
family was, it seemed, the more the members of that family
needed each other's warmth and love. Even if her real mother
turned up, B wouldn't go with her, and she could then give up
her identity as an exceptional being.

B suddenly stopped on the stairs.

"Is it okay if I go to the bathroom?"

"You just went at the restaurant. You need to go again?"

As the man spoke, he took one step up toward where she was
standing. B quickly moved up one stair from him, as if to warn
him to keep his distance.

"I'll just leave my bag here and go."

Since she had no intention of running away, B took on a dignified attitude. First, she'd run home and explain the situation
to her mother, ensuring that she'd have enough time to make
appropriate preparations. Then she'd come back and lead the
man to her home.

"Go on, then."

The man's response was reluctant. He couldn't very well follow a young girl into the alley where she was going to relieve
herself. On the contrary, it was a situation requiring him to
stand there with his back turned. B handed her school bag to
the man as if instructing him to keep an eye on it, then turned

and hastily set off down the alley that was connected to the staircase. She thought that he wouldn't be able to see the connected
side from the staircase gate where he was standing. When he'd
climbed a few stairs, however, he was at a point where he could
observe everything in all directions quite easily. B ran with all
her might. The moment she came out from the alley, gasping
for air, having run quickly around it until she was once again
moving toward the stairs, she was standing face to face with the
man, already waiting for her at the point where the two roads
met. B's entire body froze.

"Is there a washroom here?"

This time, the man didn't have a blank expression on his face.

"You are a very bad child."

He spoke angrily, not caring if he was too rough. His eyebrows were raised fiercely, his mouth twisted cruelly. All of a
sudden, he violently threw down the black bag that he'd been
carrying at his side all along; it was a threatening action, as if
he had a knife inside the bag and was about to take it out. The
staircase was on a remote alley, so there were no other people
going by. B continued to pant heavily, her mouth wide open and
her shoulders moving up and down. Her entire body trembled
as the sweat on it cooled. She stared vacantly at a point behind
the man, who was standing one stair above her. With her mouth
open and panting, B gazed up at the steep staircase continuing endlessly behind the man, and beyond that, the seemingly
close but absolutely unreachable blue sky. The next moment, she
buckled at the knees.

B's Road Home

B STEPPED IN through the gate with a meek expression on her face, as if she were entering someone else's home. Seeing her daughter with the man following closely behind, B's mother seemed to grasp the situation at once.

"You didn't scold the child or anything, did you?"

"Of course not."

The man shook his head in broad movements and even waved his hands.

"She cried a little on the way here. Maybe her legs hurt. I even bought her some *ddeokbokki* at a snack shop."

"Anyway, please sit down here on the floor."

At B's mother's invitation, the man sat on the edge of the floor, took his jacket off, and set it at his side. He brushed off his pants, his face showing comfort at having finally found a place to sit.

"It was quite a long way to your house, and the buses don't come out here either."

B sensed a slyness in the man's tone, as if he knew something more.

"By the way, your daughter seems very kind. She was worried that you wouldn't have any money, even if we came to your home."

"She worries about every little thing."

"She told me her father wasn't at home. She even begged me not to come here. She really gave me a hard time."

"I wonder why she did such a thing."

With an expression indicating the lack of importance she attached to the matter, B's mother turned toward the kitchen and asked, "Would you like a cup of tea?"

"A glass of cold water, if you have it. With May approaching, it's already quite warm at midday."

There was no reason for B's mother to welcome the debt collector. Still, if she just paid the money and was done with it, there would no longer be any need to be servile. It was an unanticipated expense, but six of the twenty four monthly payments didn't amount to that much money. Above all, it was very fortunate that they'd brought the books with them when they moved instead of throwing them out. They would have had to pay for something that they no longer possessed. When the man told her that he was going around collecting the debts from the many outstanding accounts that his predecessor in the company had left behind when he quit, B's mother even went so far as to say to him that young people really have a tough time of it. B's mother brought a small tray supporting a glass of water and gave it to the man, who set it on the floor, lifted the glass to his mouth and leaned back to take a drink; then the two discussed the special discount price at which the *World's Classics for Boys and Girls* had been purchased, acting as if nothing was out of the ordinary.

Leaning against the door to the room, B suddenly started screaming with laughter. With her hair tangled and her knees smeared with dirt, she laughed like crazy, her shoulders shaking. It was about the time when the movie her classmates were watching would be coming to an end. It would have a happy ending, of course. Even with the great number of codes to be deciphered in life, there is absolutely nothing in this world that should surprise us.

B's laughter seemed uncontrollable. Even as she hobbled into her room on her knees, dragging her dirt-stained school bag behind her, the sound of her laughter grew loud in sudden bursts. Furrowing her brow, B's mother turned her head from the man and watched her daughter's retreating figure. There were red stripes distinctly imprinted on the back of B's neck. It was clearly someone's handprint, someone with a hand large enough to wrap around a girl's neck.

How B Astonished the World

When B awoke this morning, she pulled a sweater over her pajamas and stepped onto the floor with bare feet, as usual. The first thing she did every morning after getting up was open the curtains. As she pulled them back, she wondered what kind of a day it would be. She took great pleasure in that short time she stood at the window, looking out with that thought in her mind. After closing her eyes to revel in her anticipation of what the day might bring, she slowly made her way to the kitchen to make coffee.

Even the ring of the telephone that broke the silence made B happy. Is it some unexpected news? When she got home from work, she'd open the mailbox and take out the mail, of which the first things she'd tear open were the ones whose sender or contents she couldn't guess at first glance. Though quite often disappointed, she accepted even that as a formality to getting news. She hadn't lost her fondness for the unfamiliar. For example, it was her habit to look at the car in the next lane when she was waiting at a red light, just to see who the driver was; or she'd stare at length at the not particularly meaningful emergency exit arrow whenever she went to a bar for the first time. When she went hiking in the mountains and happened upon a graffiti-covered rock, she'd stand for a long time in front of it; neither could she simply pass by an amusement park's wooden fence with a specific date that lovers had carved into it. On her days off, B liked to put on her sneakers and wander aimlessly around her old neighborhood. Then, on a late spring night, when she discovered a rusted iron door deep in the darkness of an unknown alley, she stopped and lost herself in thoughts about the world behind that door. She also thought about her family members leaving one by one and never coming back.

B's life was as ordinary as ever. She knew well that life wasn't something that turned out as one wished. But she knew that there was also nothing wrong with flights of fancy. The fish swimming quietly at the aquarium, as if resigned to their fate, enjoyed such rare and brief moments, too, when they'd leap up, twisting and flapping their entire bodies in the air. "With the whole body bound, being carried away in dark water toward some deeper, unknown darkness, such is the life of a human." B had copied this phrase from a book. Though she was being carried off somewhere in a great current, she still wanted at least once to suddenly stand up in the boat and joyfully wave her small, white hands high in the air, as if she were dancing.

B remembered standing on a long staircase that stretched endlessly toward the sky and bursting into laughter, a long, long fit of laughter, utterly unable to stop. Was it from a dream she'd once had? Even of late, she'd occasionally burst into laughter for which she didn't know the reason, just as in her dream, and the people around her would stare at her with astonished eyes.

Boundary

SINCE MORNING, THE sky had been overcast with low-hanging clouds. B turned on the headlights. There weren't many cars on the road, but the wind was blowing hard, and from somewhere, perhaps an overturned freight truck, an endless stream of colorful fabric and pieces of Styrofoam were flying around in the air. It was one of those days. The whole sky was a dreary ashen color, the guardrail was broken, and torn pieces of tire were lying here and there. A little farther on, there was broken glass scattered on the black highway, and rolling around among it, the debris of some unidentifiable object. Now and then, torn bits of polyethylene rose up from somewhere like a flock of black birds searching for food. In the middle of the road, the mangled remains of a furry animal, flat and red, caused the passing cars to reduce their speed. In places, black tire marks veered from the lanes at sharp angles. Today was one of those days.

Everyone was driving wildly, their headlights on as in an emergency, racing as if to flee the plagued and cursed city. It was a day of minds being troubled without reason and evil nightmares of the night before coming to life. What in the world happened in this city last night? B wondered. Am I at a boundary?

At that moment, rain began to pour down. One car was crossing the center line of the highway from the other side and coming toward her at a dangerous speed. B saw two large discs of light penetrating the darkened world, speeding straight at her. A wicked glimmer, as of an evil spirit's eyes; a brief whimper, momentarily portentous and suffocating, in the face of catastrophe; the hazardous, burning smell of something on fire; the piercing sound of metal striking metal; all of these struck her head painfully. B slammed on the brakes with all the strength of her entire life.

A torrential downpour from her youth appeared on her retinas. On a balmy spring day, a young B was riding on the back of her eldest brother's bicycle down a newly-constructed road. Darkness suddenly surrounded her. The sky, the most frightening and expansive sky she'd ever seen, was completely covered with dark clouds, and an unusual wind brushed against her, sticking to her skin. Her brother pedaled with all his might to get home, but the heavy rain eventually began to pour down. Her entire body was soaked in an instant, and with the rain hitting her in the face, she couldn't see directly in front of her. It became more and more difficult for her brother to pedal as his pants clung to his body. He seemed ready to abandon her to the rain and take off alone on the bicycle. B had no way of knowing what was going on inside her brother's mind as he pedaled frantically, his lips tightly shut and his face wrinkled as best he could to prevent the rain from getting in his eyes. B clung desperately to her brother's back. Just as they finally managed to reach their home, with all their energy spent making their way into the yard through the open gate, B noticed something strange. There was no rain coming down there. With the itchy crape myrtle tree and all the roses, standing in line, casually looking at her, there was her mother, standing in front of the kitchen door, trimming the tender, lustrous sweet potato shoots. Not one drop of rain had fallen in the yard. Perhaps it was a different world.

MAP ADDICT

1

HAVING QUIT HIS fifth job, B is posting on his blog almost every day. When he jots down a passage from a book he's browsing through, and then has to take a walk around his neighborhood, just for fun he takes pictures of back alleys with his cell phone camera and uses them for new posts. He works hard at digging up things like funny parodies or weird serials making their way around the Internet and linking them to his blog. But most of his posts, as you might expect, are trivial stories about him and his friends and the news he shares with them. I'm never finished work before midnight, so I often can't join my friends for drinks, but I actually prefer it this way. After my classes at the cram school are over and I get home and take a shower, I take a can of beer and sit down in front of my computer to read his posts, an indispensable part of my daily routine since I don't know when. Late one night, there was a new post titled "My Friend M is Type 9." M was my initial.

Title: My Friend M is Type 9

Do you hate traveling? Then you're just like my friend M. He thinks travelling is the most troublesome thing in the world. I've often heard that people go on trips in search of freedom, but I think that's wrong. That's because in foreign places, there is restraint and tension with everything. You have to wander around like a caveman in search of a place to eat and sleep, and you should do a lot of tiring preparation to avoid getting lost.

Above all, you have to plan out a daily schedule to fit inside a fixed framework, and M would prefer not to do this. He's afraid of adventure, has a strong aversion to strangers, and, as the "Master of Deliberation," he even has a hard time choosing from the menu in a bar. Maybe he's led his whole life without trying anything new. Aha! That's right, a typical Type 9! Like all those who aren't good at taking care of themselves, M is an expert at rationalization. If, as he insists, we are forced to experience the extraordinary and intense when we're abroad, it's to some extent part of the basic package of life, in which we're pulled this way and that every day. So there's definitely no need for us to volunteer for adventure. And meeting new people? Since there are only a few types of people anyway, isn't meeting new people nothing more than increasing the number of samples in the collection? M knows a lot of people, but because they're mostly neither close friends nor mere acquaintances, he's the type who shares his time halfheartedly.

The pictures he takes while wandering around, diligently charging his camera or changing the film in it, taking no time to sit and rest; and once he's soaked in a little of the atmosphere of his travel destination, the crude souvenirs he buys, his huge, wheeled suitcase bulging with them: M sees the belief that such things will last for a long time as nothing but an illusion. I've never seen him too concerned about pictures or souvenirs upon returning from a trip. He thinks that, despite the experiences one has while travelling, human life is actually conducted in a place called "routine," which falls into the category of the civilized present. He's thoroughly modern, an urbanite, quite a radical even among those people who prefer to stay in their comfort zones, the self-appointed "cocoon" people, don't you think? Do you know what he says about those who wander through places like India or Africa in search of primitive beauty or some lost source of existence? First, why would they go to the trouble of trying to discover something most people aren't even curious about? Second, I wonder why they go to all that trouble when they're probably not much different than me, one who reads extensively about the world at home through the Internet, not moving a single step. Whenever M is flipping through the channels on television and finds a program about, say, polar exploration, like the one titled "Challenging Human Limitations," a look of deep emotion momentarily appears on his face. It's relief at the good fortune that it's not him on the screen enduring such hardship.

Can you guess what kind of guy he is? He refuses to go hiking. He prefers to run on a treadmill at a health club. When a trip to a vacation spot is unavoidable, he never sets foot outside the comfortably-equipped condominium he's rented, so naturally he's never even considered going camping. His idea of travelling is taking a walk through the streets of Soho in New York or having a delicious caffè latte at an open-air café. So you think he has no interest at all in nature? He can't tell the difference between forsythias and azaleas, yet he's well aware that Sansevieria, which purifies the air indoors, also has a component that helps you recover from fatigue. More aspects of nature he enjoys are: healthy organic vegetables; a vast, well-tended field of grass, wet from a sprinkler; and a dazzling white ski slope spread out behind a ski house. While wondering if all of nature is no more than fantasy to city dwellers, M maintains that he's not unusual at all.

That's right. M is afraid of strangers and things that are different. He gets anxious if he's separated from the majority. For to become isolated, or in other words, to become an individual who asserts oneself in opposition to others, is what a Type 9 fears the most. Therefore, for fear of being unsightly, he prefers not to stand out, but tries to adapt himself well enough to every situation.

If you think M is a positive person because he doesn't seem to demand too much out of life, you totally misunderstand him. This type gets rid of his anxiety by plunging himself into pressing work, or latching on to unimportant things in order to avoid the burden of handling a big project. He's drawn by small returns in compensation for his inability to pursue what he really wants. Though he appears to go along with what others say, he's stubborn and defiant on the inside. He doesn't want his good mood to be disturbed by others, so he resists them by being quiet and unresponsive. Oh, and another thing. He's on intimate terms with alcohol, a characteristic common to those who want to escape life's problems. Hey, M, you're drinking right now, aren't you?

As you've probably guessed, M doesn't have many friends. But fortunately his close friends are all pretty decent guys, including me. We're knowledgeable, talkative and sharp, with excellent senses of humor. Beyond our fields of specialty, we have expertise in at least one or two other areas. One friend, a reporter for an Internet newspaper, is a music and audio enthusiast; another, who works at a government corporation, something related to culture, is so immersed in weapons and mythology that he runs three Internet websites about them. Yet another is a low-paid instructor at a cram school in the suburbs, like M, but there's nothing he doesn't know about luxury goods, wine, and movies. He's invariably the one who first attracts women when we go out drinking; but once that stage has been passed, the women will listen to all of us, even if we talk about things like classical music or Northern mythology.

Even M, who always sits quietly in the corner, isn't terribly unpopular with women. They talk about him, saying that he looks pure, or youthful; there was even one who, upon learning that he was a Korean teacher, said that he looked like a poet. M, thinking it not too intolerable to continue playing that role, fostered it and smiled gently at her. Some people say M is modest because he's always hiding behind his friends, but those people don't really know him. With a few effortless words, he can build up his friends and at the same time elevate himself along with them, which is a very clever way of disguising himself in humility. Perhaps he's rejoicing inside, having discovered a way to become accepted into the same category as his friends without doing all the work needed to become a person who attracts attention: by simply being around them, without having to go through the tiring task of maintaining an image. Because he tends to depend on his friends, it's a big mistake to expect anything like loyalty from him. He always asks them for advice and acts accordingly, which is a way to avoid responsibility.

M is the kind of person who can't live apart from his friends and the city. He's completely satisfied, even moved, when he has a chance to sit around with a few old friends, tipping back glasses of draft beer on a summer evening at an outdoor table in some corner of the city. Believe it or not, I've even seen tears well up in his eyes at such times. I mean, he gets this look on his face like he realizes that he isn't living his life in vain after all. He simply can't leave this place, not even to go on a trip.

Besides, M's constitution is so delicate that he gets diarrhea if there's even a change in his drinking water. There's a phrase long used among our friends, "the truth of the class trip photo," and even I was impressed by the image of M in each of our class pictures, his eyes slightly downcast, his uniquely milky-white face full of anguish. Do you know what M feared most about doing his military service? Not double-time marching. Not disciplinary punishment. Outhouses. And to show how obnoxious he is, he claimed it wasn't because of a poor digestive system, but because he was of noble birth. He's still renowned for not going to bathroom very often, and it has nothing to do with his perseverance, his stamina, or the volume and elasticity of his bladder. He's just picky about bathrooms. Just imagine if he went to some snow-covered pine forest in North America, like in the Rocky Mountains. He'd be thrown for a loss, unable to find a flushing toilet equipped with a bidet, having to drop his pants somewhere deep in the forest, only to end up face to face with one of the grizzly bears those parts are famous for. As a civilized being, as one who maintains the supremacy of his arrogant species, M has never thought of himself as an animal and wouldn't even think of trying to communicate with one. His knowledge of bears is slim: he knows about *Ungnyeo*, the bear-mother of Korea; he knows the value of a bear's gall bladder; and he's heard

the old story about two friends who survive an encounter with a
bear while walking in the mountains: one climbs up a tree while
the other plays dead; lucky to be alive, holding each other and
jumping for joy, they realize the preciousness of their friendship.
Poor M! It's a good thing that it's too cold for snakes to live in the
Rocky Mountains, with the endless line of peaks rising three or
four thousand meters above sea level. I heard they're all covered
with glaciers, so what if he slips and falls into a crevice and is
frozen for all eternity? Ah, but this is all pointless conjecture. M
never travels anywhere.

As you'll see in my introductory profile, I'm the complete
opposite of M: I like travelling, uncommon experiences, and
meeting new people. I'm a Type 7, someone whose head is full of
farfetched and funny ideas, someone who always need excitement.
I do have my faults: I'm a little scatterbrained, I spend a lot of
money, and I grow tired of things easily. I simply can't stand being
bored. To those who think they're Type 7's like me or Type 9's
like my friend M, please leave a comment.

While I was reading the post, the spirited beat of a Psy song was
flowing out of the computer's built-in speakers. B had even put
some cynical rap music on to "set the mood" for my upcoming
trip. As he said, I've never even taken a bus past the entrance to
Gugi Tunnel, let alone Bukhan Mountain, but I will be weaving
my way through the Rocky Mountains next week. For ten days,
I'll have to sleep curled up in a tent, cook my meals in a campsite, drive a minimum of four or five hours a day and spend even
more time hiking in the mountains, and all while traveling with a
complete stranger. I wasn't upset about B's post, of course, which
expressed in B's own way his worries and encouragement. Though
his amusing irony failed to lessen my burden and fear of taking a
trip, it at least enabled me to anticipate the particular happiness
of seeing him again when I return. Coming back—that's the only
pleasure I expect from this trip.

2

THE TIME FLEW by until two days before my departure. The most difficult thing was getting permission from my boss. Since the official vacation was only three days long, no boss would want to give a whole two weeks off to a young, inexperienced teacher. Mine, a real go-getter, established his own institute after he'd mastered the structure and system while working in the administration department of a large institute with three branches specializing in university entrance exam preparation. His had a different atmosphere than those small-scale operations run by ex-instructors who call all their friends to come and teach, creating a family-like environment. He had excessively strong convictions, and his stubborn defense of his convictions made him very authoritarian. It was customary for him to suddenly fling open the back door of a class in progress and roughly rouse the sleeping students, shouting, "Did you come here to sleep? Sleep in regular school, not here!" The base pay for teachers was only a standard amount, but the actual salaries were completely different, depending on the number of students each teacher had in his or her charge. There were some who couldn't put up with such working conditions and either quit or got fired after arguing with the boss.

It's not in my nature to take risks. "We must simply accept what happens in life because there's really not much we can do about it." According to B, this is the attitude a Type 9 takes through life. Of course, I don't approve of the education system or the system of private institutes, and I'm occasionally filled with rage and even sadness, but it's still my duty to do my best to raise my students' grades, even by one point. In modern life, complex as it is, an individual performs only a very minor function. There are others who take care of the philosophical or conscientious tasks, like worrying about the future of the human race.

A girl I was teaching ran away from home at the beginning of the school semester. I was apparently the only one she left a message for. I contacted her mother, and when she came to see me I showed her the message on my cell phone. *Teacher, I'm pregnant. But there's no one I can talk to. I don't know where to go.* When she saw the message, the girl's mother gave me a fierce look, but the only time I'd ever talked to her daughter outside of class was at a *ddeokbokki* party, and that was in the break room with several other students around. Nevertheless, the persistent and imposing mother questioned me as if I were on trial. She was bent on making me the bad guy, as if in doing so she thought she could clear herself of all responsibility for her daughter's departure. Neither the girl's feelings of loneliness and isolation in the face of an unfortunate situation from which she couldn't through her own strength find a way out, nor the fact that she could lay bare her private life to a novice institute instructor with whom she wasn't very close, in spite of her shame, seemed to bother the mother at all.

Anyway, the girl returned home safely and, because her secret was well kept, started attending classes again. Since then, perhaps characteristic of the loyalty of her age, she has consistently registered for my classes, but her grades have not been getting any better. It was later revealed that my boss had received a substantial monetary expression of the mother's gratitude. I didn't even get a word of thanks from her. To show herself as cultured and educated, she ought to have expressed her gratitude to me, but she probably didn't want to bow her head to someone who knew about her disgrace. According to B, it's not easy to find one's way in the world because the role of schools and private institutes has changed; the coordinates have been shaken so that a mother's job has fallen to a bachelor institute instructor who isn't even a proper schoolteacher.

Two fellow instructors I sometimes go drinking with late at night offered to cover the classes I'd miss over the next few days. But when I think about the classes I'll have to teach in compensation when I get back this summer, a summer which is supposed to be the hottest in a hundred years, I anticipate a living hell. My boss put off giving me a clear answer to my request for time off and kept me anxiously waiting right up until the very last moment I had to pay for my airplane tickets. I think he believes it's his own unique way of controlling his employees.

When my boss finally gave me permission to leave, my mind went momentarily blank with bewilderment and I felt a tightness in my chest. I felt like a child running at full speed up to the teacher to be flogged. Why did I try so hard to get a vacation I didn't even really want? I mean, even I know that if I said I couldn't get any time off, then Y would no longer be able to persuade me to take a trip, no matter how strongly he pushed. A lost child will take a stranger's hand when offered and desperately follow the stranger, even while crying in fear. Once again, the "adaptable person" in B's assortment of types occurred to me. No one could help but be bitter upon realizing that he's lived his life cast in a particular type. You see, even though B has claimed ninety percent accuracy with his system, there are many different standards of classification, such as blood type, birthstones, birth trees, the Chinese and Western zodiacs, and so on.

When I received a call from Y, I couldn't speak convincingly about what was on my mind. In other words, because I'm a person whose head and emotional circuitry are mixed up, I faced the moment I had to give him an answer still not knowing what I was trying to say. On the other hand, Y's voice was, as usual, full of hard-to-believe friendliness and conviction. He said that adapting to a strange place was difficult for him at first, but once settled into his new surroundings, he found that he missed his friends most of all, and I must admit that I was full of doubt when I heard this. But any resistance I had to being drawn in by him was broken down relatively easily.

"I was wondering if you'd like to travel with me," he began. "I mean, I would if I were you. Our married friends have their own families to support and are tied down by their jobs. All you have to do is show up. Hey, we should just do it. If you keep weighing your options, we'll never get together."

As I listened to Y, I couldn't help thinking about the moment we bid him farewell at the airport the year before last when he chose to emigrate after closing his failing business. All of us friends who'd come to see him off held his hand tightly and told him repeatedly to get in touch whenever he got settled and we'd definitely drop everything and rush to go and visit him.

"Hey, new hiking boots are uncomfortable, so put them on and go hiking in the mountains in Korea a few times before you come. And you'll really be glad you came when you compare our mountains to the ones over here. Not many people get a chance like this. Oh, by the way, do you know P, one of our seniors? He was two years above us at university, belonged to Mensa, exceptionally smart but a little ill-tempered. He'd suddenly stand up in the library and start yelling, even breaking a few desks there. Didn't you hear about him? I actually ran into him over here. I invited him to come with us because he's travelled a lot and would be helpful. I think you'd get along with him because you're pretty easygoing, but if you think you'd be uncomfortable, tell me. I can still tell him not to come."

"You don't need to do that," I barely managed to respond. "You said he's our senior, right?"

"Ah, you haven't changed a bit." Before he hung up, Y said in a voice filled with pride, "I didn't know you wanted to travel this badly." As I listened inattentively to him, I was thinking about the call I'd make to him in few days with an excuse, that I'd broken my leg or that my mother was in the hospital, when I suddenly saw his big, bright eyes very clearly moving closer to me.

3

THE GREATEST DIFFICULTY for people who work at night is that the rhythm of their lives differs from most others. How enormous an inconvenience it is to not be part of the majority can't be known unless it's been experienced. Once you withdraw from the many things you've become accustomed to in sharing time with others, you reach a stage of calm acceptance. When I have the very rare chance, on a day other than Sunday, to wander the streets during the daytime, I feel a sense of ease at belonging, yet I still feel like an outsider.

In the morning, when I'd usually be sleeping soundly, I arose and briefly tidied up my place. After dropping off some clothes at the cleaner's and stopping by the bank to pay all my utility bills, I went to a mountaineering store I'd been trying to find for a few days on my way to and from work. It was close to a subway station. The owner, who at first glance was obviously a serious trekker, with his darkly-tanned face and the proudly-worn mountaineering hat pulled down low on his head, brazenly scrutinized me like I was someone who'd never been near a mountain. When I told him I was looking for a pair of hiking boots, his response, as he continued with his work, expressed his disinterest.

"There are many kinds of hiking boots. Where are you going?"

When I casually told him that I was headed to the Rocky Mountains in Canada, I didn't at all expect the kind of effect my statement had.

From then on, for almost an hour, he was oblivious to the

other patrons entering and exiting the store and didn't leave my side. Needless to say, he talked incessantly about mountains. I don't know if he was typical of all serious mountaineers, but he was much more devoted to sharing his knowledge than to selling his goods. I was fine with his presentations on the origin of the Sierra cup, the various uses of a Nalgene container, which has such an airtight seal that it can be used to transport organs for transplant, and so on, but when he expounded on the ways to mend a torn tent, to cope with mountain sickness, to call for help in distress, to use a camping knife to disinfect a poisonous insect bite wound, and even the art of making drinking water out of urine, I couldn't help feeling weary. I regretted that I hadn't come with B. He didn't have a lot of mountaineering experience, but he was pedantic and had extensive knowledge on a wide variety of subjects, and within ten minutes he'd have turned the tables and started to educate the owner.

The equipment the owner chose for me was unexpectedly basic: a backpack, a pair of hiking boots, a sleeping bag, a small cup with a set of cutlery, and a container for *kimchi*, a Korean's source of strength. "Mountaineering is the real thing your body has to deal with, so you don't need a lot of unnecessary equipment", he said, and then proceeded to tell me several examples of the mettle of real Korean men who had achieved their objectives through sheer audacity and resourcefulness, even in extreme situations, without depending on such things as state-of-the-art equipment. The idea struck me that he might have been in the airborne or marine corps. He may not even have been a mountain climber. According to B's classification system, he was obviously the "old-fashioned Korean gentleman type" who "by believing the fantasy that he has no weaknesses can occasionally put himself and others in danger."

When I'd finished paying, the owner handed me two shopping bags and gave me a final piece of advice: "If you happen to meet a bear, don't forget to go into taekwondo position immediately. With such a wild animal, the battle of nerves is important.

If you scare it first, you'll break its spirit and it won't be able to attack you. I'm right, you'll see."

I don't want to see, I thought to myself.

After I got home, I started to pack. I put some first aid stuff, including diarrhea medicine, and a thick duck down parka into my backpack and tried it on my back. I decided to wear my hiking boots when I left. I put into my shoulder bag the book by travel writer Bill Bryson that B had sent through an Internet bookstore to congratulate me on my ambitious undertaking, as I was planning to read it on the airplane. B agreed to take me to the airport. When I asked him to keep my cell phone for me while I was away, he teased me, telling me to leave my insurance policy and my bank book, and to write a will, too. I used the excuse that someone could send me a text message, as in the case of the girl who had run away from home, or that I might get an important phone call. Although I was physically departing, I wasn't ready to travel, so I had to by any means necessary maintain a thin lifeline connecting my present with the existence that I was leaving behind. I didn't even say a word to my parents. They wouldn't be concerned about me if they didn't hear from me for two weeks or so. I had to ask B to answer the phone only in the case that a call came from my parents, and for that reason I had to leave my phone charger with him, too.

"Is that the only phone call you want me to answer?"

I nodded in response to B's question, although we were on the phone. "If you get a job while I'm gone," I said, "call my cell phone and let me know right away."

B answered with a wisecrack. "Yeah, I'll get a bear to tell you for me."

I checked my email one last time on the morning of the day I was to leave. There were two spam emails, a webzine from an insurance company, and an email from B. The title was "Evasion, or Advice for a Person Who Adapts."

Most people think of peace as a state of Nothing Bad Happening, or Nothing Much Happening. Yet if peace is to overtake us and make us the gift of serenity and well-being, it will have to be the state of Something Good Happening.

- E. B. White

I left my computer on until just before I left home, but no more emails arrived.

4

In July of 1983, a group of child campers led by their three teachers pitched their tents in a provincial park in Canada. At night, a 181-kilogram black bear discovered their sack of food tied up in a tree and brought it down to the ground by breaking the branch to which it was tied. When it had eaten all that, it followed the scent of chocolate bars and hamburgers and raided the tents. The sleeping children awoke and shrieked in extreme terror as they breathed their last.

A hunter in Alaska followed a bear for several days before finally succeeding in shooting it through the heart. A moment after he leaned his rifle against a tree, the fallen bear lashed out with its claws, tearing the hunter's face to shreds with a single stroke.

Two teenage boys camping in America's Yellowstone National Park unintentionally passed between a mother bear and her cub. Nothing incites a mother bear like being separated from her young. The mother bear lumbered after the boys at fifty-six kilometers per hour. The boys ran for their lives and climbed a tree, but the bear, a professional tree climber, easily followed them up and tossed them to the ground. They played dead, but it was no use. The bear gnawed on them to her heart's content.

The food cart with the Air Canada logo engraved on it was approaching, so I closed my book. Whether B was being sarcastic or not, I still believe that you should either climb a tree or play dead when meeting a bear. According to the mountaineering store owner's advice, I must change the way I think and be the first to assume an attack position. But I'm not sure I could swallow my fear of bears enough to strike an aggressive pose, no matter how dangerous the situation.

Not long ago, I saw in the news that a circus elephant, stressed out from the brutal schedule of performances, had run away. A bear, on the other hand, would never turn up in the center of a city just to get some hamburgers and chocolate bars. While aimlessly surfing the Internet, I found a series of tragic love stories about bears, in which every night a male bear leaves a private zoo to enjoy a stroll, but can't return to his cage after a negligent security guard locks the door, leaving the female bear sad. I also came across a spring movie publicity event in which three people would be picked to receive stuffed bears the size of their boyfriends simply by participating in a survey about their impression of bears. The flight attendant was standing right next to my seat. Choosing fish over beef, I wondered which choice I'd make if I were a bear.

5

ACCORDING TO THE map, Y was living in a city right along a route that passed through the Rocky Mountains. But in reality, it was a long distance from there, a full day's driving without rest. Y stressed that he was living not on a peninsula like Korea, but in North America, a continent. "Above all," he said, "when you see the Korean kids going to school here, you'll think to yourself a hundred times over, I'm glad I came." The next moment, perhaps realizing that I was a bootlicking institute instructor in the excessively competitive Korean system, he changed his tone. "But with so little stress over here, with their tension relieved, their eyes become completely glazed when they haven't been back to Korea in a few years. You know that Korean kids have a focused look in their eyes and military-like discipline." From the moment I met him at the airport, Y spoke often of the success stories of emigrants, and he always ended by promoting the quality of life enjoyed by people who go to live in advanced countries. But he lived in an apartment building on the outskirts of the city, so his circumstances didn't look that good.

There was a reason Y had told me several times to get an international driver's license before I came. His right hand was bandaged.

"How did that happen?"

"I hurt it stopping a fight in a bar. I'll have no trouble travelling, I just can't drive or wash dishes," he said, slapping me enthusiastically on the back with his left hand. P, our senior, had said that he was leaving early in the morning to come and join us. He appeared to be coming by train, even though by continental standards he lived close by. When Y handed me the car keys and told me that we had to go meet him at the train station, I couldn't help asking about it.

"He's not coming by car?"

"He doesn't drive. I told you he's a little strange."

I was in a bit of a daze from jet lag, and even my stomach was starting to give me trouble. But I held the steering wheel and kept my eyes wide open to accustom myself to the English road signs.

"It's so much more comfortable driving here in Canada where they use kilometers, instead of miles like in the United States, isn't it?" Y hit me on the back again. "About P, he's a little unique. Try to understand him, in spite of his peculiarities."

"What peculiarities?"

"In short, he can't adjust himself to society. Every time he fails at something, he leaves everything behind, even his family. Whether he's a misanthrope or what, I don't know, but he's had psychiatric treatment. In particular, he becomes violent when drunk. Don't drink with him."

I eyed the bandage on Y's hand. "Is that how you got hurt?"

Y mumbled something to himself as if to avoid answering my question. "He can memorize things like documents and account books in an instant. Memory, calculation, he's really amazing at such things. An unfortunate talent, I guess. In any case, he's not the kind of person who can live in a society like Korea's."

My first impression of P was that he was unyielding and melancholy, perhaps owing to the information Y had given me about him in advance. He was very big, a full ninety kilograms at least, and he gave off the aura of one whose body was half ablaze with glowing flames and half filled with dark, flowing water. He took no notice of me at all, making it abundantly clear that he was the leader of this excursion, the one who had planned all the routes and the schedule, and that he and Y had initially planned to go by themselves.

Our first destination was J, known as a tough part of the

Rocky Mountains to explore. After surveying the rugged mountains there, we came down to B, a popular tourist spot, seeing glaciers, lakes, hot springs, and coniferous forests along the way, before finally reaching the last stop on our day's itinerary, a small town near the border that I'd already heard about from Y. Anyway, it didn't matter. My main concern was that only one day had passed since we'd set out on this trip. When we departed in the car, Y, sitting in the back, started chatting with P, who was in the passenger's seat up front. I don't know if they were in collusion with B in Korea, but their conversation was mainly about bears.

"Bears should be hunted on downhill trails. If you kill a bear on an uphill trail, you can't take it with you because it's too heavy. For that reason, most expert hunters acquire the skill to take apart a bear into flesh, bones, entrails, and so on."

Y had even had the experience of carrying a gun along on a bear hunt. Though he'd expected a breathtaking fight like in a scene from a movie, it wasn't like that at all. The task of hiding behind a tree and waiting motionlessly for several hours for a bear, taking care to avoid even the sound of breathing, had turned out to be an extremely calm and profound undertaking. He became keenly aware of the fact that not everyone was fortunate enough to encounter a wild animal in its natural state. He was very much looking forward to both meeting a bear and not meeting one. That is, he definitely wanted to see a bear, but it had to be from a safe distance. He'd heard a story about a bear that came into the campground of some national park and demolished thirty-six vehicles because a newlywed couple had stored their wedding cake in the trunk of their car. Though bears naturally like the smell of sweet things, they're also fond of the scent of cosmetics and will pursue menstruating women. Their olfactory sense has evolved enough to detect prey even upwards of a kilometer away. In view of this, to take advantage of their sensitivity to smells, a bear repellant spray was developed. The safety of such a spray, however, is uncertain. Bears are curious creatures and may follow the scent even more persistently, think-ing, "Where is this odor I dislike so much coming from?" Y even explained, with regard to bear paw cookery, why the right paw is tastier. When a bear opens a bee hive, it uses its right paw first, and the swarm of bees stings that paw more intensively, making the quality of meat on the right paw finer than the left.

P hardly said a word. I looked at him out of the corner of my eye. With his head drooping slightly and his downcast eyes, he appeared to be dozing. For someone half asleep, he seemed to be holding his head rather stiff, and it wasn't until I glanced sideways at him a few times as I held on tightly to the steering wheel that I realized what he was doing. He was looking at a map. Each and every page of the thick map resting on his lap was curled up at the end, each corner likewise severely worn. Its condition, rather than indicating its age, showed more that it was the tortured pet of its disturbed owner. It may even have been because its owner wore it out looking for directions he was never able to find. The roads weren't even complicated enough to have to look at the map that often. On the contrary, it was a tedious route, following a highway for several hours without even having to change lanes. It was, if anything, strange for P to keep his eyes glued to the map. Ah, he's a map addict, I thought.

When he'd looked at the page spread out before him almost long enough to memorize every road on it, he began to flip back-ward and forward through the map book. With the route we'd come along so far perfectly ingrained in his mind, it appeared that he intended not to stop at that, but to completely famil-iarize himself with the geography within at least two thousand kilometers in all directions from our current location. He didn't look at the outside scenery at all. His attention was focused only on estimating his present position on the map. The direction in which he was headed, his destination, and such things didn't appear all that important to him in comparison to the task of checking his current coordinates. I wonder into which num-bered type B would classify him. No matter how different and unique a person P was, B would eventually discover a category to place him in.

It was the morning of the next day when we reached the final town before entering the district of J. As soon as we turned off of the highway, our eyes were met with beautiful snow-capped mountains continuing on without end. Since I'd been looking at the densely snow-covered scene for several hours, with the snow in layers looking like the pattern on the sides of the dark mountains of rock, I no longer thought it necessary to travel to our destination. I'd already seen the Rockies to the point of disliking them, and I was seriously sick and tired of driving. I stopped the car in front of a general store, and Y went in to buy some firewood, water and canned beer. I sat at an outdoor table in front of the store and lit a cigarette. The image of P browsing through an assortment of maps in a display stand next to the counter caught my eye.

The weather was very fair. I felt like I'd entered a brightly-colored picture postcard. In the clean air, the first relaxing cigarette I'd had in a long time didn't taste bad at all. I was looking around for a place to throw away the butt when Y approached and pointed to the garbage can with the characteristic hook hanging from it.

"They make them like that so the bears can't open them. Bears can't bend their claws inward, so the lids have hooks on the inside like that."

Y looked excited as he took a bear repellent bell from his backpack and tied it onto the zipper of his windbreaker. He then hung a small whistle on the end of a long string around my neck and told me rather grimly that singing in a loud voice is another way to drive away a bear.

"If you happen upon a bear, the best thing to do is pretend not to see it and keep walking. That's what the bear wants, too. It won't attack if you don't provoke it. Try to go into taekwondo position or something and you'll be dead on the spot."

I watched carefully as Y took his cell phone from his pocket. I felt uneasy when he eventually turned it off, saying that there was no longer a signal. When I called Korea the night before, B informed me that my cell phone hadn't rung once.

"Everyone knows that you left on a trip."

But his words weren't very comforting. Overhearing my conversation with B, Y asked sarcastically, "You still call your friends first whenever something happens?"

He didn't ask to talk to B. At one time, B, Y, and I were inseparable, but at some point Y went his own way. It may have been after I'd become active in the administration of an Internet literature site for which B was the system operator. I think it was then that I chose B over Y to be my coordinates.

6

MOST PEOPLE PREFER the convenience of a city. Still, I've never heard anyone say that they feel out of place in nature. Whether they like it or not, humans possess a feeling of closeness to nature and react instinctively to living organisms. Everyone wants to make enough money to be able to live in a house with a big garden and a nice view, from which they could look at flowers, trees and water. I've never imagined a situation in which nature could cause suffering. That was before I saw the mountains around J. They weren't at all like the scene from a postcard. The desolate gray mountains of rock, veiling the sky like an enormous cement wall, called to mind spine-chilling terror more than majesty. With the sunlight hurting my eyes like a baby just out of the womb, and the fallen tree trunks submerged like the bones of a herd of dead animals in the streams that came into view at every bend in the path, it all suggested some cursed time from the beginning of the world. There was nothing of the motherliness or intimacy or harmony that is associated with nature. My gut feeling is that our use of the word "nature" undoubtedly refers to what nature was before we'd chosen a name for it.

The campground P had reserved for us was infrequently visited, an isolated place situated in the deepest part of the mountains in the J region. During the nearly hour-long drive there from the town of J, we did not meet a single car coming in the opposite direction. There were several campsites positioned here and there in the dense forest of the campground, like the tunnels in an ant hill, but we were the only campers. While P was gone to the bathroom, Y used his left hand to halfheartedly help me unload our things from the trunk of the car.

"It's P's style to plan out a route like this," he said. "The usual route is to pass through the tourist area around B before coming up to the J region. But we're doing it backwards, starting with J and then going down to B. Instead of climbing a slope of gradually increasing intensity until the summit is reached, it's more his style to leap from level ground up a steep incline to the top, and then to make his way down slowly."

"What the hell kind of way is that?" I replied angrily.

P had been so absorbed in looking at the map he got from the information booth at the entrance to the J region that we very nearly entered without getting a parking permit.

We'd planned to go hiking as soon as we unpacked our things and set up the tent. The mountain had a gentle slope, so it wasn't as difficult as we'd thought to climb up above the tree line. But there was something frightening I couldn't have anticipated. It was the silence. I'd never imagined such a harsh and isolated reality like that, dozens of kilometers of the natural world full of all kinds of life in every direction, but no humans at all. Consequently, the moment I saw a sign indicating a hot spring, I nearly collapsed on the spot from the feeling of relief that we'd reached human civilization. I didn't feel like going one step farther. But the 'hot spring' was nothing but a stagnant pool that the native Indians had used a long time ago. No matter where I turned, there was only a feeling of the dreary alienation of time and space, as well as silence. From time to time I felt a chill, as if a dark shadow was sweeping between the trees, causing me to freeze several times in my tracks.

Following behind me, Y soon began to clap his hands, telling me not to worry about my back. On top of that, he even blew his whistle. Then, perhaps feeling reassured, he walked up to P and began speaking to him.

"Surely there won't be any bears on this path, will there?"

P replied with no emotion. "To bears, walking along this path would be no easier than walking through the woods."

After a brief silence, Y spoke again.

"Were there lots of strawberries this year?"

"Why do you ask?"

"I've heard that bears appear more frequently in years following poor strawberry yields."

Soon I too was walking closely behind Y, waiting in expectation for P's response.

"June is summer in the city, but in these mountains the snow melted a few days ago and spring is only now just beginning. For bears waking from hibernation, this is the time to eat mainly grass in order to expel the feces that have been in their intestines for so long. With so many nourishing herbs around, why pay any attention to the burdensome flesh of animals?"

His tension finally eased, Y started to make jokes.

"Man, if I could communicate with bears, I'd let them know how tough and distasteful my flesh is."

P turned and glanced at Y, and then replied, as if to a triviality, "That would have been possible 180 million years ago. Back then, bears and humans were the same organism. Eukaryotes stemmed from one ancestor population. In the distant past, flowering plants, insects, and humans were all one organism."

"Oh, is that so?" Y said quickly, giving me a wink. I think it was a signal that he'd heard enough. 180 million years. It wasn't, after all, a period of time that a being who didn't even live a hundred years could imagine. But P didn't care at all what other people thought. Units of time from the ancient past began to spill from his mouth.

"Evidence for Ice Ages over the 'most recent' two million years has been revealed. The oldest Ice Age occurred 57 million years ago. During the last 42,000 years, the earth has shifted between glacial and interglacial periods four times, while the longest Ice Age began 2.5 million years ago and ended 10,000 years ago. The Rocky Mountains were formed mainly in the late Jurassic Period, and even as far back as the Paleozoic Era, when magma permeated deep into the Precambrian crust. At that point, sea creatures climbed onto the mountains and became fossils. The rock we're currently standing on was formed between 1.1 and 2.7 billion years ago."

Y, who had been waiting for the opportunity, finally interrupted P.

"Well, I was in Italy, and because all the buildings and statues were from before Christ, I felt so insignificant. Now I come here and everything is in tens of thousands to millions and billions of years."

"So what? In fact, even the genes in your body have been around for ten thousand years," said P, using the map he was holding to block Y from walking ahead of him.

Though we hadn't discussed it, P was in charge of cooking and Y dealt with the fire. Washing dishes alone at the unfrequented campground's public sink was my part. Additional odd jobs were left to me, too. These were things Y would've had to do if I hadn't been there. After finishing the dishes, I took the *kimchi* container, the camping stove, and our emergency food supply and put it all into the public food storage locker, in accordance with the bear warning notices advising not to leave any leftover food on the tables or in tents. The storage locker, secured tightly with iron chains and a second locking device, was shamefully empty. I went to the bathroom and quickly washed up, all the while feeling anxious that a dark shadow would suddenly burst in through the door. When I returned to the campsite, I found P sitting alone in front of a roaring fire drinking a can of beer. In his oversized, rough hands, the shiny silver beer can looked very small. The brand was "Wild Rose," produced in a small local brewery. I was exhausted and wouldn't have said no a beer, but, remembering Y's warning, I crawled into the tent. Y was already fast asleep in his sleeping bag.

When, half asleep, I opened my eyes and glanced at my watch, the glowing hands indicated eleven o'clock. Feeling a little strange, I lifted a corner of the mosquito netting and looked outside. Unbelievably, as if morning had come, it was light out. The campground was frighteningly quiet, as if someone were plugging my ears, even though a few other groups of campers had arrived late that afternoon. P was in the same position, still drinking beer. There was a map open on his lap. It was like watching a screen after pressing the mute button. P sitting there quietly with a beer in his hand, his enormous back, the vigorously blazing fire next to him, it all felt like a scene from a dream. There were numerous "Wild Rose" cans scattered around his feet. I sunk back into my sleeping bag.

I don't know why I opened my eyes again. I think it was the sound of footsteps. I distinctly sensed something approaching the tent. My mind raced, urging me to ready myself, but strangely I couldn't move a muscle except to breathe. I think I even heard Y make a low moaning sound. With my whole body stiff and cold sweat dripping off me in my sleeping bag, I waited in terror as the unknown creature's dull, heavy footsteps moved closer. All of my senses became focused at once into my ears, and my heart was beating so fast it was painful. I closed my eyes tightly. But at the moment it seemed that the footsteps would stop in front of the tent, they passed and gradually receded into the distance. Certain that they were indeed growing fainter, I remained frozen for a while in the darkness and silence. I don't know how much time passed. An indescribable sustained howling sound, undoubtedly animal-like, neither from nearby nor from afar, could be heard. Was it a bear? When I murmured the question, Y made a rustling sound in the darkness, whispering, "It's P." Not long after I heard him turn over onto his side, he was snoring once again. I listened for a while for more sounds from outside. I finally realized that it was still light out after eleven o'clock because of the northern latitude. In some places in the world where the sun stays up all night, surely there are those who remain awake, unable to sleep. I suddenly felt a vague sadness for every being still awake at this hour. I wanted to be a part of that group, whatever it was. Once again, the animal-like howling cut through the stillness.

7

Though I drove for hours each day and then went trekking in the mountains without even taking time to rest, I didn't get tired. With bandages on the places where the new hiking boots stripped the skin off my feet, I became accustomed to walking this way and that on the mountain trails. My stomach, too, gave me less trouble than I had feared it would, possibly because we made our own food. One time we encountered rain while we were in the car. The moment the fist-sized raindrops started to hit the car window, one after another bursting with a firecracker-like popping sound, I reflexively held up my arm to protect my face. But it stopped in an instant. Whenever we took down the tent, it wasn't easy for me to have to see all those wriggling insects gathered underneath, trying to share in the warmth of my body. Every time we finished eating, before I could even enjoy the feeling of being sated, let alone drink a relaxing cup of coffee, I had to perform the annoying task of getting up to do the dishes. As the days went by, however, that too became routine. Perhaps it came as a consequence of the inexpressible dignity of living a life within the simple rhythm of eating and traveling and walking and eating again and sleeping.

The sad scene from the animated movie *Leo the Lion: King of the Jungle*, in which Leo says, while eating a deer he has hunted, "I wonder why we have to eat only meat," is only human interpretation, and has nothing to do with nature. Sitting next to the still breathing deer, eating into its internal organs, the infant lion's mouth is completely covered with blood. He looks no different than an innocent child eating noodles, with sauce smeared all over his face.

P wanted to do everything alone, wholly according to his own methods. He disliked it if we offered a different opinion about a destination, or pretended to know in which direction we were headed, or even cut onions for him when he was cooking stew. He was a person who moved only in accordance with the map inside his own head. Still, that didn't mean he followed his determined path with error-free precision. On the contrary, he was ridiculously ignorant in terms of the basic common sense that everyone had and would approach a problem in an unpredictable and complicated way, like looking up the meaning of the words "next" and "door" in the *Encyclopedia Britannica* and the *Oxford English Dictionary* and the *Annals of the Joseon Dynasty* in order to visit his next door neighbor. His way of thinking was by ordinary standards completely inconsistent, so it was difficult to know what he was going to think or do next. But P had no doubt at all that he was following the simplest and most clear-cut route. If there were actually someone who looked up to P and wanted to follow him as a leader, it wouldn't be easy for that person to curry favor with him because it's impossible to understand what's going on in his mind.

P's abnormal sleeping habits were indeed another of his idiosyncrasies. Instead of sleeping in a tent, he preferred to lie on the bare ground and fall asleep looking up at the sky. He liked it because he could see the stars and, in particular, feel a breeze brush against his face. When he took off all his clothes and crawled naked into his sleeping bag, he looked like a wild animal in its fur. One night, I awoke from a dream in which I was being chased by an enormous shadow, and I didn't know if it was the shadow of a bear or P. Suddenly gripped by a strange feeling, I stepped outside the tent, expecting to see P lying on the ground with his sleeping bag pulled over his head, but he wasn't there. Maybe he became a grizzly bear when the hour was late, like a frog becoming a prince. But there he was, stumbling out of the forest's early morning mist, looking not unlike a drunken man who, having collapsed and fallen asleep at the very place he chose to urinate, was awoken by a chill and was now making his way home. The only difference was that instead of wearing clothes, he was wrapped in his sleeping bag. Judging by the scratches and blood on his face, it was clear that he'd tripped and bumped into a tree or something. He did occasionally hurt himself like that, but he had no violent side to him at all. Y's warning about him being a vicious drunk was probably just hot air.

Some of the campsites we stayed at were enclosed in wire fences with a weak electric current running through them in order to prevent wild animals from entering. In those places, I still cleared the area around our tent every night, taking care not to miss a single grain of rice, and faithfully put our left over food inside the public storage locker, all in an effort to safeguard against a bear attack. I considered myself to be solitary and a little stronger than before. I crossed the dark forest without a flashlight to go to the bathroom, and although I'd still get startled if some rustling sound came from the next stall, I'd calm down right away. Even if the feet I saw under the door of the next stall somehow belonged to a bear, and the bear asked me to share my toilet paper or grumbled about the inconvenience of not having any hot water, I don't think it would be enough to frighten me out of my senses. It became my habit, or even my obsession, to think about bears. I was walking once in a valley in the pouring rain with my duck down parka on, and when I eventually took it off, the sudden thought of a bear who like me was wandering around without rain clothes, getting wet, made me feel indescribably refreshed. When I rode a snowmobile to the top of a glacier, I imagined myself soaking my feet in the melted ice water with a bear. I even thought we could share some meat or fish.

The J region didn't attract a lot of tourists. Consequently, a number of cars lined up along the side of the road indicated that people had stopped to look at the wildlife. There were lots of caribou and deer, and occasionally even coyotes. One time

I saw a Rocky Mountain goat standing perilously at the edge of a cliff on a high, snow-capped peak. Staring silently into the distance, its white beard fluttering in the wind, it looked sublime, like a monk or a philosopher living existentially in a polar region. But we didn't see any bears. Though Y had been complaining constantly about that fact, he gradually seemed to grow indifferent to bears.

On the last day, Y, P and I drank until the campfire burned itself out. Wherever P happened to sit, the old map was always the very first thing placed on his lap.

"After carrying that thing around all this time, haven't you memorized it yet?"

In response to Y's wisecrack, P smiled sheepishly, saying, "It's different every time I look at it."

I asked Y, "Is it okay for you to drink alcohol? You'll likely get some inflammation on your wound."

"It's practically healed, anyway," he responded, bravely unraveling his bandage.

I'd already sensed not long after our trip began that there was something business-related Y wanted to discuss with P. A long time ago, when it was trendy to give one's friends nicknames beginning with "Master," B's nickname for Y was "Master of Tricks." B would have been able to ferret out the numerous lies Y had potentially told me. While opening his can of beer with his right hand, Y said to me, "Let's make a bet. Whether or not a bear can open a beer can." Just then, from the part of the campfire where the wood was piled up, a spark suddenly jumped up with a crackle and soared toward P's cheek. I wondered if he'd be transformed from a map addict into a bear if fire touched him. It was the last of my bear-related fancies. The trip was almost over. The only joy I could experience from it was approaching.

8

Title: Rocky Communication

Thank you for waiting so long. This is the news from my friend M, who went on the most enjoyable trip in the world. You're all aware, aren't you, that he left his cell phone with me? Well, a text message arrived for him yesterday. Quickly opening it, I saw that it was from his credit card company, notifying him that his card had been used to make a purchase. Do you know what this means? That's right. It means M used his credit card in Canada. Eighty-five dollars. Clearly for alcohol, right? Be happy, everyone. He's finally joined civilized society.

But it's a little strange. He hasn't called yet. I wonder if something happened in the forest. Since he hasn't bothered to contact his friends, maybe he married a bear.

Title: P's Coordinates Originate from O

My friend M hasn't changed a bit. The very next day after he got back, he returned to the city and his friends and drank draft beer until dawn. He checked his cell phone for missed calls and messages as soon as I gave it back to him. If I ask him, "Were you expecting a call?" he'll play innocent and say, "Absolutely not." In fact, he may even be waiting for ex-girlfriends to call him and ask for his forgiveness for the wrongs they inflicted upon him. He has no backbone, so he's always quick to forgive. I told him that his mother called while he was away, but he didn't seem particularly happy about it. I mean, I even lied for him, which wasn't easy for someone like me, telling her that M was on vacation in Anmyeondo with a bear. "Didn't anything happen while I was gone?" That was all M seemed curious about. His ulterior motive was to hear that his friends missed him, but we all knew him for such childish schemes. Poor M. He was lured to the Rockies, only to suffer great hardship, and he can't even count on his friends for confirmation of their friendship. M repeated the same question three times, so one of his friends finally said something. "While you were gone, New York had its worst ever power outage." "That's last year's news," said M with a laugh of resignation. Anyway, for the first time in their lives, the people of New York saw a sky filled with stars. Just like our friend M.

The one change in M is that he no longer fits into the Enneagram classification system. Looking at him now, he's too careless in many aspects of his life, and a little too relaxed as well, to be an accurate and diligent Type 9. Did his personality change after seeing so many stars in the Rockies? Man, I too am beginning to think that the zodiac is a more reliable system of classification. For stars really are humanity's oldest coordinates. You all remember the definition of coordinates, don't you? "A number or pair of numbers describing the location of a point, P, relative to the point of origin, O, on an axis." We learned that in math class. In other words, "P's coordinates originate from O." Since M is the type to always have a need for coordinates, I wonder if he's been driven by difficulty with bears in the Rockies to plot coordinates for them. But don't place too much confidence in coordinates. The coordinates of the human race have been shifting continuously since the beginning of recorded history.

Humanity is now at the apex of an evolutionary period extending over three billion years. Since the Cretaceous Period of the Mesozoic Era, when the bodies of our ancestors surpassed a weight of ten kilograms, we've been rapidly evolving to the point where we now have very large brains. And in the natural world, different species don't encroach on each other's territory, so their probabilities of survival are higher. Take birds, for example. Certain birds are predators, while others are teeth cleaners. Some have beaks to catch insects, some have beaks to eat seeds, and some, like hummingbirds, have beaks to drink nectar from flowers. Penguins, living alternately on land and in the sea, and ducks, moving extensively between land, water and air, rarely encounter one another. That's because they want different things. Diversification reduces competition, which is nature's way of allowing many species to coexist.

But you know what? Army ants eat different groups of ants, and king cobras prey on other snakes. Bull sharks eat small sharks, and tiger sharks and hammerheads will brutally devour their own kind as well. What does this mean, you ask? It means that the condition under which members of the same species or group don't view each other as their own kind and are able to eat each other is a stage in the accomplishment of diversification. In the natural world, if you want to become one of the surviving strong, you have to see your own species or even your friends as outsiders, even so far as you are able to prey upon them. A tad spine-chilling, isn't it? It must sound cruel, even tragic, but it doesn't go beyond the individual's strategic instinct to survive one way or another. Anyway, I wonder what M would do if I told him to eat me. His eyes would light up and he'd chew me out, exclaiming, "How could I eat a friend?" He can't. I think we have to find different coordinates for M. Though it's a tad cliché, life finds a way somehow. Having friends that are always hanging around you makes it difficult for other friends to get close. And when would we accomplish our historical directive to evolve if we stuck only to our current course?

Was I a little too talkative today? Actually, I don't think I'll be able to post very often from now on. I've been enjoying myself for a while now, spending almost all my money, so it's time for me to crawl back to work. Another reason is that the hot summer has passed, and fall has come to cool off my head. The brutal, sweltering nights went on for several days in a row, and then early one morning, I felt an unexpected chill in the air and, pulling up my blanket, realized that fall had suddenly come. At that moment, didn't you mutter something like this? "Ah, fall comes suddenly, just like the age of thirty." Until now, this has been B, a pro-social and optimistic Type 4.

9

THERE'S A STORY that I didn't even tell to B.

It was the day Y wanted to stay at the campsite because he wasn't feeling well. I'd have preferred not to go hiking with P alone, but it was unavoidable because I had to drive the car. P invariably led the way with map in hand. Passing by at least three frozen lakes, we arrived at our destination just after noon. It was a beautiful forest, exceptionally serene in the absence of visitors, with streams of clear ice water running through the dense grouping of coniferous trees. The sunlight pouring down through the branches extending straight out from the trees reflected on the spider webs contained in the empty spaces between, making it look as if there was a sparkling silver bicycle wheel rolling on each branch. I felt like my whole body was gradually being saturated with cool green water.

Following silently behind P, I eventually realized that he was no longer looking at the map. It meant that the trail we were following was already off the map. Then I noticed that I was treading on natural soil and not a path created by Parks Canada.

"This isn't the hiking trail. It's not even on the map. Let's go back."

"I enjoy the pleasure of following roads not taken by others."

P even broke into a smile. With a sudden feeling of anxiety at the idea that I'd been seduced by the scenery into venturing in too deeply, I turned and looked behind me. Though it was broad daylight, the shadowy darkness of the forest was everywhere; we could see nothing if we strayed even a little from the path. Just like Y had done on the first day of the trip, I had no choice but to follow close behind P.

"There aren't any bears, are there?"

"You shouldn't feed wild animals. They stop trying to find food on their own and start taking it from others. Or they beg for it. Try releasing a trained bear into the wild. Unable to adapt, it will inevitably tag along behind hikers in search of food. People and bears are the same. You mustn't try to befriend them. Standing in opposition to others is the way to survive."

"Is it true that you come to the mountains quite often?"

"I like the wild. You never know what's out there. A world of only people is too plain. Humans are uninteresting because they adapt too well. That which only adapts can't evolve."

"Do you mean to say that rebels are more well-disposed to evolution?"

"In a tropical rainforest, there are millions of arthropods we know nothing about, and millions of invertebrates in the depths of the ocean. Like us, they too are evolving."

I got the impression that P was not very accustomed to conversation. He seemed only concerned with what he himself was saying, even if he didn't completely ignore the speech of others. It was quite cold, though the forest was still shrouded in the stillness of midday. I saw a phantom sweep by like a dark shadow deep in the forest, and when I'd finally forgotten about it, it passed before my eyes once again. I tried to keep the conversation going.

"What evolution are you thinking about?"

"Everything becoming something different, that's evolution. Humans are supposed to feel uneasy about differences and should reject those who aren't the same. But in the wild, those who are different are respected. Out there, being different is the way to survive. With different habitats, different prey, and different enemies, only such different beings can coexist peacefully."

"Why are you so obsessed with maps?"

P snickered.

"The easiest quadratic equation for me to solve is from

reading coordinates. When the origin O is certain, you can use it to find the location of P."

"When you find P, does it show you the direction you should take?"

"No."

The smile was suddenly gone from P's face. His focus moved to a point somewhere beyond my back.

"There is no such thing as a correct direction. Humans simply have to continue searching for it."

With his eyes still fixed behind me, P slowly lifted his finger to point at something, and only then did I turn around and look.

The needles on the pine trees were a glistening green, and the dark shadows of their densely-growing trunks stretched out lengthily on the carpet-like grass beneath. In the midst of them, a patch of long, beautiful brown fur was moving slowly. A face with dark eyes and a long muzzle was pointing toward us. The bear stopped and focused its gaze as if it had discovered something. I could hardly breathe, but I couldn't take my eyes off the animal. Stopping at a yellow dandelion, it quietly extended its neck as if to smell the flower and, with an bored look, broke it off. I felt a shiver. Life in its natural state, its beauty and spontaneity and majesty, overwhelmed me.

10

THE PEOPLE RETURNED to the city, their holidays at an end. It began to bustle once again, and the neon signs of bars remained lit late into the night. I was kept very busy for a while after I came back from the Rockies. Vacation was the peak season for private institutes. Also, the institute I taught at in the new area of the city, unlike those in Gangnam, focused on comprehensive classes. Everyone knows that it's much more effective to move from institute to institute, taking only those classes needed for college, rather than to suffer the restriction of a single comprehensive curriculum. But to do that, mothers have to drive their children all over the place, and such a thing is possible only for the wealthy of Gangnam. It's a distressing situation, but nothing can be done about it. People are inevitably raised in different environments.

One day after classes, the girl who had run away last semester was waiting for me.

"Are you troubled that your grades haven't improved?" I asked.

"No, it's not that," she said, looking intently up at me. "Teacher, I don't know where to go today. Instead of *ddeokbokki*, would you mind buying me some alcohol?"

After some hesitation, I gave her the web address to B's blog.

"If you go there, you might be able to find the direction you should take. You could say that my friend's posts are a map, in a sense."

"I can't use the computer at home. My mom cut the Internet connection."

"Then ask your mom to buy you some alcohol."

The girl grimaced.

"I really don't know how I should live my life."

Without responding to her, I started to walk away. It was a good day for a walk. The girl glared fiercely at me, but she didn't follow. In the empty late-night streets of the city, autumn was just beginning. You don't know how to live your life? I'm over thirty, and I still don't know. The wind was cool, and stars were showing here and there in the night sky.

Not long ago, something happened at the Baker Lake Resort campground in Canada. An enormous bear with beautiful brown fur was discovered dead drunk. Thirty-six empty beer cans were scattered in the vicinity. Park supervisors presumed that the bear broke into the campers' food storage locker and opened the beer cans with its claws and teeth. All of the empty cans were the "Wild Rose" brand, a local beer. The supervisors woke the bear and drove it away, but the sober bear returned that night in search of more beer. Efforts to lure the bear with donuts and honey were of no use. In the end, they were able to trap it using two cans of "Wild Rose." The bear, driven deep into the forest, was given the nickname "Refined Drinker." It didn't drink any of the other brands of beer found in the storage locker. The bear's drinking capacity couldn't be determined, however, because there had been only thirty-six cans of "Wild Rose" stored there.

As I walked alone, passing a convenience store with a group of people sitting around a table out front, I muttered to myself: "Ah, on a night like this, a night when all my friends are sleeping and I'm walking the deserted streets by myself, an autumn night with stars in the sky and a cool breeze blowing, I wish I could have a drink with the bear."

PRAISING DOUBT

1

ON A TRAIN, a group seat was an area where four passengers had to sit facing another. Because of the size of the discount offered on buying those four seats, it was common for traveling strangers to pool their money and buy tickets as a group, usually over the Internet. Yoojin had been standing in front of the ticket gate for fifteen minutes, waiting for the other three. The tickets were issued in one sheet, so passengers with group tickets had to get on and off the train together. They were disposable travel companions, never having seen each other before, never to see each other again.

A man in an olive green baseball cap approached Yoojin and asked, "Did you buy a group ticket to P?" Soon after that, two painstakingly dolled-up, rather vociferous high school girls came over to where Yoojin and the man were standing side by side and asked the same question. "Are you the people who bought the group tickets?" The four of them stepped in through the ticket gate together like a nicely wrapped gift set.

The man offered a window seat to Yoojin. The high school girls sat down in the seats opposite. From the way they carried on the moment they were seated, it was obvious that their destination in P was a concert by a Japanese singer. Across the aisle in the other group seats was a young couple with their two young girls. They were twin sisters wearing the exact same pink sweaters and pleated wool skirts. The mother, having warned the twins not to swing their legs, pulled from their feet shoes identically adorned with ribbons.

"Are you on a business trip?" The man eyed Yoojin's formal

attire.

"No, it's for my friend's wedding." Wanting to take a book out of her bag, she answered tersely, not turning toward him. He made no further attempt to strike up a conversation. When he reached into his own bag, pulled out a book and set it on the table, a perplexed look flashed across Yoojin's face. It was the exact same book that she had been planning to take out and read. Leaving it in her bag, she leaned back in her seat and for the first time took a sidelong glance at the man's face in profile. For some reason, she was very curious about where he'd bought that book.

"Every time I see twins, I have good luck", said one of the high school girls.

"Have you ever seen an egg with two yolks? Sometimes there are even two chestnuts in one chestnut shell. I heard that's a sign of good things to come. Is it?"

"When I cross at a crosswalk, I only step on the white lines. I heard that's really good luck."

"No, it isn't."

"You know when you get stopped at a railroad crossing, when that red light is flashing? I heard that if you see the passing train, you'll be lucky."

"I think somebody just made that up because it's a pain to wait for the whole train to pass by."

The two high school girls chattered on about different signs of good luck until well after the train had departed from the station.

Yoojin, having briefly dozed off, opened her eyes at the sound of an announcement over the loudspeaker. On the opposite side of the aisle, the twins were causing a commotion, trying to find their shoes so they could get off. When the train started moving again, the four seats opposite were empty. Yoojin inclined her seat and leaned her head back, though she didn't think she'd be able to fall back to sleep. S's wedding ceremony was tomorrow. She'd received a call from S to come and spend the last night of her single life together, and the first thing that came to her mind was the big bookstore where they used to meet. It was there she'd purchased the book the man in the seat next to her was reading. She was living in a high-rise apartment building then, in a new area crowded with them.

2

Yoojin stepped into the café a little early for her appointment. The man had arrived first and was waiting for her. He attracted her attention immediately, even sitting off in a corner. When she'd seen him a few days ago, he'd seemed like a pretty boy, wearing a brown, wool-lined leather jacket with a big wool collar, and inside it a hooded sweatshirt displaying the logo of an American university. Now, in a neat black jacket and an olive green shirt, he looked a bit like a different man. He somehow, though clean-cut, gave off a dark and cynical impression. His face remained abnormally still even after Yoojin had approached and was standing right in front of him. His eyes were focused on something else, as if he didn't recognize her.

"Am I not the one you came here to meet?" she demanded, stubbornly refusing to hide her displeasure.

The man lifted his head and looked up vacantly at her. He glanced at his wristwatch. "You're ten minutes early."

"So there's something wrong with being early, it seems."

"No. I meant I didn't recognize you because you didn't come at the right time."

"Then I'll go sit somewhere else for ten minutes until you can recognize me. There's no reason for two strangers to sit together."

Maintaining his composure, the man nodded his head slightly. "Miss Yoojin Lee, you're right. We are strangers."

"If we're strangers, then how do you know my name? And that I have an appointment here in ten minutes?"

"My brother told me."

"What are you talking about you brother for? We won't even

know each other for another ten minutes."

"Miss Yoojin Lee, the person you came here to meet is actually my brother," he said, adding a moment later, "I'm his twin."

On his face there rose a polite expression, like a request for understanding. It was an expression that could be used to tell lie upon lie.

"Something urgent came up, so my brother said he'll be a little late. He asked me to come in his place to deliver that message. He doesn't know your phone number, so there was no other way he could contact you. Fortunately, my office is in this area." He smiled faintly. "When some unexpected trouble arises, everyone wants safeguards. But this time it's nothing to fret about."

"The two of you are identical twins?"

"We have the same DNA. We're destined to pass this same DNA on to our own children. Even our mother can't tell the difference between us when we are sleeping in our pajamas. But anyone close to us can tell us apart if we move or start to speak. You could say that our individual identities become obvious through our lifestyles. Even cars that are identical when shipped from the factory become different, depending on each individual owner. That's to be expected, isn't it? Though we were born from the same egg, my brother and I are two very different beings. Our parents used to say that we were like an angel and a devil with the same face. But that was when we were in our teens."

The man had finished his business, thought Yoojin, so she couldn't understand why he didn't get up and leave, or why he was going on about his personal history. Furthermore, it was unnecessary for him to keep insisting that he wasn't his brother: at the moment no one wished it more than Yoojin herself. Still, he gave no indication that he was planning to leave anytime soon.

"Inside their heads, people have their own systems of analyzing information. In other words, through their thought processes they deal with impending matters judiciously and selectively. The thought process, however, is made by a system of subjective memories. That means it's far from objective truth. Because of this, much more unexpected happens in this world than expected. What do you think about that?"

"Well, I could care less."

"Let me reiterate. Consider the five senses and the mental capacity of a human being. Whether we're conscious of it or not, the amount of information we're presented with on a daily basis is enormous. People know far more than they think they know. But if we could recall everything we know, we wouldn't have any control over our lives. For that reason, people selectively accept only that which is appropriate for their own thought processes. That's precisely how a system of memories is made. It's kind of like a manual for making judgments. But the problem is that the manual is extremely subjective and partial. When something arises that can't be analyzed with the manual, people usually just label it chance and that's the end of it. In reality, there is an inevitable cause and effect relationship in all the happenings in the world. The information that the manual needs to help you determine the relationship between cause and effect is missing."

"So are you saying that I'm now involved in some cause and effect relationship that I don't even know about? You make it sound so complicated."

"You think you met my brother by chance, don't you? Or, to use a more arbitrary term, destiny?"

"Then you're saying it was some kind of scientific phenomenon?" She'd been quietly listening to him, wishing for the unpleasant sophistry to come to an end, but his audacity went too far. She sat up in her seat and straightened her back. "According to you, humans unconsciously expose a vast amount of personal information, right? I too cannot even guess how much information about myself I've made known, nor to whom. To people who live in the same neighborhood, who have the same job, hobbies, or a similar routine. Anyway, you're saying I've unknowingly encountered a large number of people in many different places, and the people I've met have defined information about me by their arbitrary standards and are keeping it in their own system of memories. That's what you're saying, isn't it? Even though you didn't recognize me when I came in here, it seems that you know more about me than I thought. Let me hear something else from your abundance of information about me."

Suddenly the man turned toward the counter and signaled to the server with his hand, but he didn't order anything, which Yoojin thought odd. The server, who had been instructed by the man not to interrupt his conversation until he was called for, came and asked him if he was expecting more guests. He thought for a moment and answered no. The server was about to ask something further, but instead, shrinking under the man's icy demeanor, he bowed submissively and returned to his work. Yoojin wanted to ask him if his twin brother was coming then, but she also kept quiet, not wanting to provide him with something he'd expect.

"A few days ago, a delivery service brought you a box of apples," the man began. "Although you hadn't ordered any apples, you accepted it because the address and the name were plainly yours. You must have thought that someone had sent it to you as a New Year's gift. So you ate some apples. Then, the very next day, a man rang your doorbell. You know who that was, don't you?"

"Another one of your acquaintances?"

He ignored Yoojin's sarcasm. "It was my brother. He asked if you had the mistakenly delivered box of apples, and you, having opened it, must have been at a loss. But my brother didn't look at all like a rude or dangerous guy. No, he was just the opposite. Most women like him. He was tall, looked naïve, and he dressed smartly, too. He gave off an intellectual air and was, in short, just the type of man you desired. When you invited him to come in out of the cold, he even politely declined at first. After he sat on the chair you offered, he displayed his sense of humor by saying he wanted an apple instead of tea; you apologized and said you'd reimburse him, but he said he didn't need to get the apples back because you'd already given him an apology, using the homonym of apple (*sagwa*) and apologize (sagwa) to make a joke.

"Although it was a brief meeting, you were probably thinking throughout the conversation that you and my brother had many things in common. Seeing your bicycle leaning against the wall in the entryway, he started to talk about the numerous places he'd traveled on his mountain bike. You listened to him with keen interest because you like traveling. It was the same with the Matisse painting. He asked you whether you'd been to the San Francisco Museum of Modern Art, and you were surprised, saying you'd bought the poster in the souvenir shop at that very place. You added that you couldn't forget about the splendid brunch you'd had in the museum's outdoor cafe. Then my brother said it was indeed one of his favorite places and that he used to go to school in that area. Surely you remember his cell phone ringing then. His ring tone was a John Lennon song, just like yours. But that's not all. Later, when you cut up an apple and he speared a piece of it with his fork, you realized that you were both left-handed. Also, you both were Sagittarians, and you had the same day planners. Then you went on about how Hemingway and Picasso had used the same brand of planner.

"My brother stood up to leave at the proper time. And as he was going out the front door, he said, there's an Irish pub I go to occasionally. Would you like to go with me some time? He also wanted to treat you to dinner at the Indian restaurant next to the pub, if you happened to like curry. Both the pub and the Indian restaurant were places you liked. When coincidences spring up, people wonder, is this simply chance, or is it a sign of destiny? You opted for the latter. The series of events that day were enough to hypnotize you into thinking of my brother as your destiny."

Yoojin was about to reply, but the man went on.

"My brother told you why the box of apples was mistakenly

delivered to your house, didn't he? The Everville complex where you live has two buildings, Building A and Building B. Before Building B was built, the name of Building A was just Everville, with no letter attached to it. So out of habit, the original residents of Building A don't specify which building they live in but continue to use just Everville on their address. For this reason, all mail without a building letter written on it is invariably delivered to Building A. You live in Apartment 805 in Building A, and my brother lives in Apartment 805 in Building B. When he told the delivery service his address, he said simply 'Everville Apartments', and so the box of apples was delivered to your home."

"You mean he had the apples delivered to my place on purpose? Why would he go to that kind of trouble?"

"Please just listen. You were so embarrassed because you'd already eaten some of someone else's apples, and perhaps more importantly, you lost some of your composure because of your feelings for my brother. Didn't you check the shipping label on the box? Wasn't it strange that, apart from the address, even the name was the same?"

"Are you telling me that your brother already knew my name and address?"

"Don't you remember seeing the name Yoojin Lee somewhere recently?"

Of course she remembered.

She believed everything had begun one afternoon last year when she was with S. They'd met at a big bookstore around Kwanghwamoon. Yoojin bought a novel and a collection of prose to read while she was alone over the holidays, and S chose *New Year's Fortune through Horoscopes*. They also bought a couple of the planners that were on sale as they passed by the stationery section. Then they had lunch at the fast food restaurant attached to the bookstore. S went on enthusiastically about her plans to go skiing with her boyfriend. They talked about their hopes for the New Year. When Yoojin said that she wanted most of all to have a boyfriend, S clapped her hands playfully. S and Yoojin were the same age, both born in December under the sign of Sagittarius. A short time earlier while shopping for books, they'd leafed through the one that S eventually bought and had read that Sagittarians of their age would meet their destined love in January.

The name of the translator of the collection of prose that Yoojin had bought that day was Yoojin Lee. It wasn't unusual for her interest to be piqued when she encountered someone with the same name as hers. In her school days, she found someone with the same name in her class nearly every year. Among people she didn't know very well, having one thing in common was enough to begin a friendship.

"You may never have thought of Yoojin Lee as a man's name. According to your system of subjective memories, Yoojin is a woman's name. But my brother and I were born in the U.S. while my parents were studying there. Eugene is a man's name there. There's Eugene O'Neill, Eugene Levy, Eugene Smith. If you stop and think about it, you too have processed the name Yoojin as a male name. Your system of subjective memories simply didn't select the data."

"Do you call it subjective judgment when someone associates herself with her own name?"

"It's not that black and white. It's a question of the parts and the whole. In this world, nothing happens without a reason. The world is completely governed by order, though it's not something you can see. That's why rational forecasts are possible. The study of statistics proves through numbers that something that appears to have happened accidently is in actuality a necessary result. As the number of samples becomes greater, even extremely rare events occur more readily. So the more predictions you make, the higher the probability that you'll be correct. It's a common trick used by those with 'supernatural' powers to make as many predictions as possible."

"Sorry, but what does that have to do with me ignoring the

possibility of Yoojin Lee being a man?"

"Your name is Yoojin Lee, the one living in the building next to you is Yoojin Lee, and the name of the translator of the book you bought is also Yoojin Lee. How can something like this have happened accidentally?"

"You say accidental, and it's precisely that. It's coincidence, isn't it?"

"We give significance to chance occurrences. Someone has the same birthday or is wearing the exact same clothes; you keep hearing the same song in different places, or you read a book with the same idea you were thinking; you and another person say the exact same thing simultaneously, or every time you look at a clock, the hour and minute hands point to the same number. Things like that. But the probability of such phenomena occurring is merely low. The problem is that people want to believe there is some special significance. For this reason, the art of detecting coincidence has been continuously cultivated through natural selection because the ability to discover meaningful connections between various events has served as an important advantage to the survival of humankind. Your case is no exception. You think something happens repeatedly by chance and you attach meaning to it, as if it's destiny."

"I'm sure you'll be able to find the inevitable causal relationship somehow."

"If my brother had known everything about you beforehand, fabricating coincidence after coincidence between you and him wouldn't have been difficult. The destiny you thought was there didn't really exist after all. You must be familiar with the famous scientist's words, 'God does not play dice.'"

"For that matter, it has been concluded that God does play dice, hasn't it? Of course, the argument that he doesn't is still out there. But if there are times when he plays and times when he doesn't, it means that he does play. Like you said before, the question is about the parts and the whole, isn't it? I also believe scientists. They continue to make new discoveries and investigate the relationship between cause and effect. But with new discoveries perpetually being made, there's still so much in this world that remains unknown. We have a tendency to put our faith in recently discovered laws, but that doesn't mean we can call them absolute laws."

"If we don't make judgments and preparations using laws, the world will be thrown into chaos. Are you saying we should live without concern for anything? Things like weather forecasts, traffic information, marketing, and criminal investigations are possible precisely because we have analysis and predictions based on laws. Art creates tension by betraying the established patterns of human thought, just as jokes can be made when they run contrary to the patterns that everyone anticipates."

"The other day when I was driving my car, I called the police traffic division to ask why the road was blocked with so much traffic. It was simple. They said it was because there were too many cars. It was only by chance that there were so many cars. Crime is the same. Scholars usually search for the cause in personality disorders, family problems or the pessimism of society, but in reality random crimes are being committed more and more frequently for no reason at all. It's meaningless to apply laws there."

"If people don't think rationally they will go through life constantly being deceived. Just like you."

"Have I been deceived? I'm sorry, but except for you and your brother being twins, there isn't anything you've told me that I didn't already know."

"Does that include that my brother's actions were deliberate?"

"What if those deliberate actions were just what I wanted?" Yoojin jutted her chin out a little. "I'm not blaming you for misjudging me. You attempted to reconstruct my existence and judge me by trying to collect the missing information, but you have no idea what goes on inside the head of a person like me. I'm the kind of person who doesn't follow the laws you understand so well. I'm not an impetuous person who's so easily convinced that there's someone who has the same name and address as me. I'm very good at remembering people's faces.

"I first became aware of your brother standing behind me when I was browsing in the bookstore. He waited quietly until my friend and I moved away from the bookshelf. I thought he had the same interests as me. I also sensed goodness in him, not like other people who push their way in just so they can grab the books they want. I caught a quick glimpse of his face out of the corner of my eye when I turned to go to the counter. That's how I was able to recognize him when he came and sat down at the table across from my friend and me when we were eating fried chicken. So, you see, I was in fact secretly watching him.

"He didn't seem to be listening to our conversation. He was lost in thought, quietly eating his hamburger. You think I became interested in him because he was well prepared with knowledge about me, but that's the hole in your theory of everything being connected through cause and effect. Do you understand? Even if your brother and I'd had nothing particular in common, I still would have come here to meet him. You probably wouldn't understand, but those decisions were made when I first saw him."

"If you're interested in my brother, there must be some reason. Perhaps he looks like someone you know. Or maybe you feel he showed you some unexpected kindness."

"Aren't the events that occur purely by chance the real driving force behind the world? If everything that happens can be put in some presupposed category, you can scarcely call that life. I don't know if you've heard what John Lennon said. He said that life is what happens while you're busy making other plans. Your brother didn't plan anything. Why do you think I was so surprised when I saw your brother standing outside my door? That's right. It's unusual for a guy I met by accident in a bookstore, a guy who didn't leave my mind for several days, to live in the next building and even have the same apartment number. But I became suspicious when I discovered that his name was also the same as mine. I started to wonder if your brother had intentionally found out my name and address, and that he'd had the apples delivered as an excuse to come to my place. I was also worried about my friend making such a racket in the bookstore that day. In your words, I spread around too much information. I'd gone straight home from the restaurant that day, so I wondered if he might have followed me, or even if he'd known who I was from the beginning."

"That's it exactly. You're living in an area full of high rise apartments. You hardly see any people on the streets even though there are so many of them living in the area. It's a system in which you are completely isolated from your neighbors. Instead, there are closed-circuit cameras everywhere to control and care for you. Even in moments when you feel that you're completely alone, you're actually sharing your time and space with countless unknown neighbors.

"I told you that rare occurrences can happen more frequently as the number of samples grows. For example, it seems like coincidence for you to meet some woman who's buying tampons on the same day as you in the same small corner store, but such a thing would be commonplace in a big supermarket. Your part of the city, overcrowded with apartment buildings, is more like a big wholesale warehouse than a neighborhood. My brother may have met you anywhere, a coin-operated laundromat, a convenience store, a bar, a real estate agency, an ice cream shop, an auto body shop. He might have stepped out of the way when you rode by on your bicycle. He could have made eye contact with you when you both ordered the same dish in the curry restaurant across the street, or perhaps you had appointments at the same time and walked one after the other to the subway station. Maybe you've seen my brother around once or twice, so that made you think he looked familiar."

"It's possible. Let's say that the things he did, like adjusting his ring tone to match mine, or revealing himself as a Sagittarian, or pretending to be left-handed, could have been based on information acquired thanks to my friend's big mouth. And he'd also know that I ride a bike or that I like curry if he happened to see me in the neighborhood. But was it necessary for him to deliberately have a box of apples delivered to me and pretend it was a mistake? I certainly wouldn't have rejected a conversation with your brother, no matter where or when he wanted to talk to me."

"It wouldn't have been as natural as going in search of a parcel that was delivered to the wrong address. The possibility of you letting a complete stranger that you met somewhere earlier in the day into your home and then serving him apples is much smaller."

"That's precisely the difference between someone like you and me. I'd rather entertain doubts about cause and effect being in too perfect accord. The events of that day were just like that. Although they themselves were extraordinary, every situation was too natural and there was nothing at all awkward about your brother's manner. It was like skillful acting. In fact, it gave me doubts. What's this? This is all going the way I wanted much too naturally. I feel like I'm getting mixed up in something. You know, suspicions like these. What do you think I did in the end?"

"Did you let my brother deceive you because you wanted to make him your destiny? It's called the Barnum Effect. The world is full of naïve people who are unwilling to accept their own fate and want to attach reality to it by force."

"I asked your brother directly. Did you follow me home from the fast food restaurant and sneak a peek into my mailbox? Of course I needed courage to do that. Your brother is obviously more likely to be the victim of stalking than me. But as I've told you many times, I don't believe that life moves in perfect accord with laws."

"I wouldn't have done that if I were you. It's not like him to tell the honest truth about everything. He's very good at deceiving others."

"Your brother told me how he found out that there was another Yoojin Lee living in Apartment 805 in Building A. The conversation we had was nothing like the one I just had with you, in which you reconstructed everything in terms of cause and effect. You came here acting like you know all there is, but you don't. You've been insisting that your brother's memories are different than mine. Memory is not as simple as DNA."

"You talk as if you know my brother better than me. Let me hear what he said about how he came to know that there was a Yoojin Lee living in Apartment 805 in Building A."

"One day, your brother had a few drinks and drove back to the apartment building drunk. He went out to drink more after he parked his car in the parking lot."

"He's an alcoholic."

"But the next day, when he went down to the parking lot, he discovered that his car had disappeared. He clearly remembered seeing the familiar logo printed on the building when he had driven into the lot, but despite all his efforts, he couldn't find the car. He informed the police, but he still hadn't heard anything after several days."

"I know all about it."

"Your brother went drinking again a few days later, and afterward he was on his way home, this time by taxi. He put his hand in his pocket and discovered that his cell phone was missing. Thinking he might have left it in the pub, he told the taxi driver to turn around and go back. But they got into a big argument. The driver was treating your brother like a drunk, speaking abuse and insults."

"It's not news that he sometimes has fights."

"Your brother stopped the taxi on the road and got out, and the angry taxi driver swore at him and sped off. Right after the taxi left, he realized that he'd left his wallet on the back seat. He waved his arm frantically toward the taxi, but it was no use. He ran after it, saw the license plate number and reached into his pocket for his cell phone so he could report the incident. Of course, there was no cell phone. It had really been a horrible day for him, but that wasn't the end of it. He said it was as if he'd been driving on a highway with countless cars and, suddenly wrapped in some unknown terror, felt like getting out from behind the steering wheel and running away."

"Didn't he say that he sometimes suffers from panic attacks?"

Yoojin thought for a moment. The look on the brother's face as he'd told her about it came vividly to her mind.

"He looked around only after the taxi had completely disappeared from view. The streets and the buildings were all unfamiliar to him. There was no way to tell where he was. The late hour made it frighteningly dark and desolate. Off in the distance was a high-rise apartment complex with windows lit here and there, massive, like a mysterious castle. He turned and, with no particular plan in mind, unable even to venture a guess at his current location, started walking in the direction the taxi had gone. Without his cell phone, he couldn't even call anyone for help. He came across a public phone booth and was happy for a moment, but he didn't have a single coin in his pocket. As someone so accustomed to living in the city that it permeated him to the core, he was a complete stranger to such a situation. That an isolated state like this lay hidden behind the everyday, with only a single layer between, horrified him more than anything. He walked slowly, like a wind-up doll, with scarcely a thought in his mind, and as he made his way home, walking through the night for two hours, he was overcome by the sensation that his insides were slowly emptying.

"When he arrived at his building, he was completely worn out and had grown faint. But then a strange thing happened. As he walked up through the parking lot, he noticed that his lost car had returned and was sitting right there. Anyone would've shuddered with fright then. But for your brother, I think it was much more intense. He told me that a sudden awareness came to him, causing him to physically tremble. He realized that it was not his car that'd disappeared, but he himself."

"I must reiterate: my brother has somewhat of a mental problem. His head is full of indecipherable garbage that disregards the rules of rationality. He has nothing but childish, disjointed ideas. He's been taking medication for a long time, you know."

"I trust my own feelings more than the information you've given me here. In your language, isn't that the art of finding advantage in life?"

"Anyhow, are you saying that the returned car told my brother about you? Did it come back with a mouth?"

"Your brother said that when he saw his car back after its disappearance, he felt as if he'd returned tired and worn out from a long journey. Before taking the elevator up to his apartment, he went over to the nearby mailboxes and casually took out a few pieces of mail addressed to Yoojin Lee. Then he went up to Apartment 805 and entered the number on the keypad at the front door. It wouldn't open, though he tried several times. He stood there for a short time with his forehead pressed against the cold, locked door. It was the strangest night he'd experienced in his entire life. Haven't you ever had that kind of moment? Surely everyone has at some point, in a single spontaneous, bizarre moment, shuddered in panic at being trapped in the narrow gap between presence and absence? Your brother too would have been seized by a sudden fear in front of the locked door, as if he'd been lost in space and was returning to a residence that was forever lost to him, as if he'd momentarily come upon a time and place that didn't exist in this world."

"As if he'd been compressed and was experiencing a black hole firsthand."

"With cold sweat dripping from him, your brother examined the mail he was holding. Only then did the letter A for the building on the address catch his eye. That's how it happened. In a drunken state, he had originally parked his car in the Building A parking lot and then, only half-conscious as he was that night, once again mistakenly went to Building A. He didn't even realize that he was in a different building because the two are twins, built in the same form with the same materials. He put the mail back in its proper place and moved his car to the Building B parking lot, but he was unable to sleep that night. He did not even entertain the idea of going to see the Yoojin Lee in Building A. Your brother isn't foolish enough to drag nighttime events into the daytime."

"What you're saying, then, is that the person named Yoojin Lee living at the same address in the very next building, as well as the mistakenly delivered apples, was all just coincidence? Fine. It may be coincidence that you and my brother are both named Yoojin Lee. But do you think it's just chance that it's also the name of the translator of the book you were reading?"

"That occurred to me after your brother left. I thought a lot about us bumping into each other in front of that same book-shelf. So I have to ask: is he by any chance the translator?"

For the first time in a while, a smile appeared on the man's face. "I can't blame you for thinking that. Especially after seeing the American university sweatshirt he was wearing."

"But he probably isn't. Even though the book was lying there on my desk, your brother didn't say a single word about it. I guess it's possible that he didn't see it, though."

"How could I have known that you had a book translated by Yoojin Lee if he hadn't seen it? You know, the more I listen to you, the clearer it becomes. You really don't think much of my brother."

"You sure go out of your way to make my decisions for me. And you're completely wrong again. Why would I have even come here if I didn't like your brother?"

"You didn't come to see my brother. You came to see Yoojin Lee."

"Is there a difference?"

"Of course there is. Yoojin is not my brother's name, it's mine. The translator is me, too. The mountain bike, the univer-sity in San Francisco, the taste in planners, and even the sweat-shirt, they're all mine. My brother has spent nearly his entire life with me. This time, too, as he has countless times before, he was merely doing an impersonation of me. Like my parents used to say, I'm the angel and he's the devil. He does as he pleases, behaving recklessly, childishly, irresponsibly. Even when he ordered the apples, he had to use my credit card because his own won't work. Your hostility should be directed toward him, not me. You've got the wrong person. The one you thought was your destiny is actually me. I hope you're not too embarrassed."

"You seem to think that if I'd been in the same situation with another person, identical in appearance, I'd automatically have the same feelings for that person. If it'd been you and not your brother who came for the apples that day, I'd never have come here. It's not objective information that moves people. It's unexplainable sensations and feelings. Do you think human existence can be understood through closed-circuit cameras in a crowded city? Sure, it's possible nowadays to be informed about all the happenings around the world through an Internet connection without leaving your dark little room, but there's no way to get a real sense of life there. No, I'll wait in this café until the person I came to meet shows up."

"Even though the truth has been revealed?"

"Other than your brother having a twin like you, none of this new information has put me off."

"Not even him deceiving you into thinking he was Yoojin Lee?"

"Now that I think of it, he never actually said he was. Contrary to your analysis of cause and effect relationships, perhaps he took no pleasure in posing as you? You know, something else just occurred to me. If I'd asked your brother if he was Yoojin Lee, he would've told me he had a twin, and then today's unpleasant conversation wouldn't have been necessary. Oddly, though, I didn't ask him about that. Don't you think it's the unexpected, the things that depart from the script and the rules, that make the world go around?"

"I don't really care whether you wait for him or not, but he won't come. I told him I'd confess everything to you."

"Why do you need to make a confession when your brother did nothing to deceive me? By asking you to come and tell me he'd be late, wasn't he in effect saying that he didn't care if you told me you two were twins?"

"You still believe he's going to come, don't you?"

With that, the man suddenly burst into loud laughter, causing Yoojin great distress.

3

S was still in the emergency room, but her face was calm, her treatment having been duly administered. Yoojin had hurried over and looked rather worn out. In the country hospital that took in injured skiers from the resort, people were running this way and that. Four skiers, including S and her boyfriend, had been hurt in a ski lift accident. They could hardly be called hospital patients, though, judging from their clothes or the topics of their conversation or their boisterous behavior. S talked continually about the accident. In the morning, from when her shoelaces kept coming undone, the ill omens began. At the ticket office and in the bathroom, she'd been cut in front of several times as she stood in line, and she'd even lost her hat. She'd twice spilled coffee from a vending machine, and she'd fallen down three times on the slopes trying to avoid the lingering beginners. S's boyfriend was worried about her and suggested that they go back to their lodgings and come out to ski again at night, but S insisted on giving it one last go. On their way up the slope on the ski lift, the accident occurred. S looked tenderly at her boyfriend leaning back on the bed opposite and then bent toward Yoojin. She spoke in a low, whisper-like voice. "Sagittarians are supposed to meet their destined loves in January. I think it's come true."

"Did you meet someone new at the ski resort?"

"No. You see, all this time I've been sure that I love my boyfriend, but I've had doubts about whether he's truly my destiny. If my true destiny were to come along in the meantime, and I didn't realize it, what then? I'd be letting the real one slip away. But going through this accident with him, I feel more certain than ever that my boyfriend is the one I'm destined to be with."

S beamed at Yoojin. "Soon something good is going to happen to you, too, Yoojin. You're a Sagittarian, you know."

"I think it already has."

Yoojin told S about the mistaken delivery and the man she'd met because of it, as well as the argument she'd had with his twin brother.

"Sagittarians are very argumentative, after all," S said. "So what did you do? Did you wait for him to come? Did you actually meet him?"

"I was going to wait for him, but then you called. I rushed over here. I guess I could have asked that unpleasant man for his brother's phone number, but with you in the hospital, I was too preoccupied to think of it."

"My destiny's arrival has prevented you from meeting yours."

"If it's really meant to be, I'll meet him again, I guess. Maybe at a bookstore or a fast food restaurant."

S abruptly shook her head. "No. Something's just occurred to me. I remember that man. While you were browsing the shelves, a bookstore employee led him over to where we were. She pointed in your direction. 'The book you want is over where that woman is looking. It's our last copy.' He stood behind you, waiting impatiently for you to put the book back, and I got a really clear look at his face. He was definitely not the same man who was sitting in front of us at the restaurant."

"You saw him too? So I wasn't the only one interested in him?"

"Is it wrong for me to look at an attractive man who's just the right age? I still hadn't found my destiny by then, you know. Anyway, both men were wearing black coats, so there was a similarity. And they were both good-looking. But the man at the bookstore had a bit of a pudgy face. The one at the restaurant was the slender, pretty-boy type. I guess the man who came looking for the apples must have been the second one, judging by looks. He wasn't at the bookstore. I guess he just saw that book sitting on your desk and mentioned it to his brother because he'd translated it."

"So you're saying that the man from the fast food restaurant and the man who came to my apartment are the same person?"

"Think about it. A man appeared at these four places: the bookstore, the restaurant, your apartment, and the café. Except for the twin brother at the café, you think they were all the same guy. So that makes two different men. But if I'm right, and the man you saw at the bookstore was a different man altogether, then there were three men in all. And you don't even know for sure that the one from the fast food restaurant was the same guy who came to your door. The four men might have been four different individuals right from the start."

"And if you include the translator Yoojin Lee, that makes five people altogether. Imagine that. Until I found out about the twin, I'd actually thought that all five were the same person."

"Still, it's strange. If there really was a mix-up with the delivery, then there has to be someone living in Building B with the same name as yours. But didn't you say Yoojin Lee's brother lives there?"

"Do you think the two of them live together?"

"Have you ever seen a pair of twin brothers walking around the neighborhood together?"

"No. But even if I had, I could've forgotten all about it. I could just as well have passed right by them unaware."

"According to what the one said, the probability of either of them running into you in the neighborhood was the same. So even if they switched places, his logic is valid. It's kind of unusual, too, to know about something in such great detail unless you've actually experienced it. It's all so well constructed, but for some reason it's just too complicated, don't you think? It would be much more convincing if there was just one of them, not two. Is it possible that there were no twins to begin with? Until you've seen the two of them together, how can you be sure about this twin stuff?"

"I really got the impression that they were two completely

different people. Were they?" Yoojin furrowed her brow. "If there was only one, then why would he have made all this up?"

"That I don't know. In any case, the more you think about clear and obvious matters, the more you delve into them, the more confusing they become. Even you and I have different ideas, and frankly, everything that the twin brother said to you could be true. There were no inconsistencies in it, at least."

"True enough. And I really do think I saw twin brothers around the neighborhood."

The two women considered the matter carefully. Everything in doubt had to come to the surface.

"I just thought of something. The day you moved in, another moving truck was over at the next building. Weren't there two really good-looking guys unloading that truck, and didn't we keep staring at them? They looked exactly alike."

"And there were those two men we saw at the curry restaurant. Don't you remember? We whispered to each other about them, wondering if they were friends or brothers. They looked a lot like each other."

There was a knock at the door, and a nurse stepped into the room. The conversation broke off there. With the nurse was helping her to sit up, S made a final suggestion. "How about paying a visit to Apartment 805 in Building B? See if either of the twins lives there, or both."

Her body already trembling with anxiety, Yoojin took a step backward when she heard those words. A single cry shot out of her mouth: "Never!"

S and the nurse stared at her in surprise.

The book translated by Yoojin Lee was a collection of prose written by a British doctor specializing in neurology. It was a story about neuropaths existing outside the framework of social norms, and one of the chapters dealt with twins between whom the boundary was indistinct. The twins would occasionally play-act, with one in the role of good and the other of evil. In accordance with their needs they'd become one person or two, and they'd often exchange roles. They made their own secret place where they could frequent each other's existence as if it were a simulation of the world, all the while thinking, I'm an imitation, a shadow, and my life is somewhere else, at a different place.

Yoojin couldn't forget what the man who came to her apartment that day had said. "The world truly moves as it pleases. It is full of filth and hatred and hopelessness. I sincerely believe that it makes no difference how we live in this uncaring world. Who cares what I am? Do you think that everything moves according to some meticulously constructed script? If so, then maybe I'm a rabbit who doesn't hop along with the lines."

4

Yoojin was sleeping heavily. The announcement broadcasting the arrival of the train at the terminal station woke her. Casually turning her head toward the aisle, she drew back in surprise. The twins she thought had already gotten off the train were back in their previously-empty seats across from her. A closer look, however, revealed that they weren't twins, but sisters who appeared to be three or four years apart in age. It wasn't the first time that Yoojin had mistaken friends or siblings of similar age for twins.

The high school girls were still chattering away. They were talking about the upcoming concert.

"Our seats are on the side, up on the second level."

"We'll still be able to see the stage all right, won't we?"

"I hope so."

"I just have to see him giving me the V sign."

"What souvenir are you going to buy?"

"A t-shirt or a cell phone strap, but only if I can find something pretty."

"I'm definitely going to buy a concert program, even if it's not pretty."

The man sitting next to Yoojin asked the girls who they were going to see. They exchanged glances, and one of them asked him stiffly, "Do you know any Japanese singers?"

"No, I don't. Actually, I like the Korean singer Eugene best."

"Do you mean Eugene the woman or Eugene the man?"

"Is there a man, too?"

"There's Eugene from S.E.S., also known as Yoojin Kim, but there's another singer, a man named H-Eugene. His real name is Yoojin Heo, but I heard that Eugene is his American name."

"American name?" The man was about to say something further to that, but changed the subject instead. "About this Japanese singer you're going to see, what's so good about him?"

"His songs are really good. Everything about him is great. What makes him even better is that you never know what he's going to do next."

"That's like the survival tactic of the rabbit."

"What's that?"

"The moment a rabbit detects an enemy, it invariably starts to run. But it doesn't follow any rules. It runs around arbitrarily, here and there. Because its movements can't be anticipated, no strategy can be applied to catch it, right? If it ran according to a script, it would be understood by a fox or a hawk and would be caught and eaten every time."

One of the high school girls asked, "If rabbits run around like that, without any rules, couldn't some unlucky ones accidentally run toward their enemies? Then wouldn't they be super easy to catch and eat?"

The man suddenly laughed out loud.

The girls resumed their own conversation.

"I heard that two others in our class have the same birthday as me."

This time, too, the man cut in.

"When there are kids in the same class with the same birthday, it's easy to think that there's some special significance. But in a class of forty, when you first consider the probability of two people having the same birthday, it's one in ten. At least three people could have been born on the same day. In accordance with the laws of algebra, mathematicians have calculated that probability to be as high as one in two. What I'm trying to say is that even when you meet people for the very first time, you'll always be able to find a few things that you have in common. We even found something in common, talking about the name Yoojin."

To avoid getting dragged into the conversation, Yoojin turned her head to look out the window. At that instant, the train entered a tunnel. The scenery vanished and the window became a black screen. It reflected the face of the man sitting next to her, who was looking at her from behind her back. In the blackened window, their eyes met. On the man's baseball cap was the logo of an American university. S will be married tomorrow, she thought. Though convinced of her love for her boyfriend, S had felt uneasy about her inability to determine with any certainty whether he was truly her destined love. She thus accepted the fateful accident at the ski resort as the signature of destiny. The horoscope that Sagittarians would meet their destined loves in January had proven correct for S. The man who'd visited Yoojin's apartment was also a Sagittarian. Had he too met his destined love in January?

YURI GAGARIN'S BLUE STAR

1

LONG AGO I used to jump out of bed as soon as I opened my eyes. I'd never lie there gazing at the sunlight coming in through the curtains, or bury my face in my pillow and roll around on the bed. I wouldn't even let my eyes linger on the framed picture of my family hanging on the wall. But when I wake up these days, the clock on my night table has barely reached six o'clock. Even if I don't hurry, I still have enough time to exercise at the health club and have a simple breakfast of coffee and a salad before I go to work. Doing only what's absolutely necessary keeps my daily routine reliably consistent.

For a while after my wife took our two sons to America for their education eight years ago, I drank heavily every night. The company was expanding, so being called out to discuss business over drinks on a nightly basis was unavoidable. Nevertheless, I invariably arrived at the office on time the following day, with my body and stomach in good enough condition to work. I don't drink so much these days. Sure, I've reached an age where I need to take care of my health, but the real reason for my temperance is that I've simply had enough of going out. The formalities I had to go through to meet new people, and then to become comfortable them, were not worth the gradually decreasing amount of new information I got from them. It's like people who fully understand what's going on inside each other's heads, sitting together sharing short-lived, trivial topics of conversation. I thought I'd found the right way to use my pent-up desire when I decided that all young women looked unconditionally beautiful.

After that period passed, I began to get tired of frequenting hostess bars and playing games with young women, and as I became sensitive to noise and even grew to dislike the sound of other people's voices, I reached a stage where I felt comfortable spending time alone. On nights when I couldn't sleep, I'd take a shower and then drink alone, a glass or two of whiskey with ice. The following morning, I'd often discover a glass full of cloudy liquid on the table. I'd have poured myself a drink, then simply forgotten about it and fallen asleep. For months now, the clock on the wall has been ten minutes slow, but rather than fix it, I simply add ten minutes when I read it.

I don't know how long it's been since I began to think of this world as nothing particularly remarkable. No matter what happens to me these days, I see it as something I've already experienced. The news, gossip from around the neighborhood, it's all like that. My job is the same, too, for there's practically nothing in my work that's beyond my capabilities. The outcome, good or bad, doesn't deviate much from my expectations. And it's not just with work, but with people as well. People I meet for the first time inevitably resemble others I've met in my life, so it becomes easier to judge them. Getting used to living in the world may involve having a formula. That is, a kind of manual for life. Everything, no matter how complicated, becomes simple when it's put into the formula. It's the same with time. When I open a new day planner filled with dates and empty spaces, I feel like I have many unknown hours ahead of me. But if I start to write in my schedule, the planner is split up into pieces, and from then on it becomes a daily routine with which I'm all too familiar. Whether this approach is praised as good management or denounced for being too conservative, I don't care. With it, the world's affairs don't surprise me anymore, but I've become somewhat apathetic.

Many areas of my life have already been settled. There are almost no variables now, at work or at home. That doesn't mean that things like bankruptcy or divorce will never happen to me. It means that I'm the kind of person who wouldn't change much, even if such things did occur. I can no longer change who I am, so things like passion and a spirit of adventure become unnecessary, and I spend no more energy maintaining the status quo. Those who have reached a certain point will no longer be able to draw mystery or the unknown from within themselves, even though they're closer to a state of perfection. They have no fear, but no excitement, either. It's neither unhappy nor happy.

2

THE AIRPORT WAS filled with people coming and going. Standing amid the noise and commotion brought by all kinds of aircraft intersecting in chronological order, I had the sensation that life rolled along only a fixed path, like the earth revolving on its axis. I considered even the act of coming out here today to see J off as something that'd been arranged a long time ago. J looked like he usually did in the office, with his cotton jacket and his camera bag with many pockets, and even his fountain pen with the white ice cap symbol on it, stuck into the uppermost pocket. But his complexion was noticeably pale, and his protruding brow ridge was casting an unusually dark shadow upon his two eyes below. His lips were thin, like those of a recovering patient. When his eyes met mine as I stood waiting in front of the departure gate, he pointed with his finger toward the smoking room. Behind its glass walls, several men with resigned looks on their faces were silently exhaling puffs of smoke.

When we'd finished our cigarettes, J slowly took his boarding pass and passport from his jacket pocket. As he made his way through the screening checkpoint to the departure gate with a heavy, awkward gait, he didn't once turn to look back. I stood there for some time, even after he'd completely disappeared from my view.

Not long after I'd paid the airport parking fee and passed through the tollgate, a bridge came into view. I pulled over to the side of the road and turned on the hazard lights. Cars were going past at high speeds. The sea water was rolling in little by little, making exquisite patterns around the pilings under the bridge. I took J's pack of cigarettes and lighter from my pocket.

"Here, you take these," he'd said.

"Why?"

Regardless of J's determination to also quit smoking when he left, there was only one cigarette remaining in the pack. Lighting it, I opened the car door and got out, the spring wind dispersing the smoke as it passed through my fingers. Just then, a huge object caught my eye, flying above my head, far up in the sky. It had a cumbersome silver belly like a man-eating shark and menacingly glittering wings. I sensed the indifferent majesty of a transcendent being. It was the first time I'd seen an aircraft flying in the sky so near.

My body trembled lightly, as if I'd been stung by a piercing beam of light. It was because of the wind. The same wind also took J's cigarette, which had turned to ash, and cast it into the air without leaving a trace.

My attention was drawn to the chairs in the office, empty because it was lunch time. A chill hung in the air of the recently vacated room, the computer monitors flickering meaninglessly with a bluish light. I passed the orderly arrangement of ground glass partitions and entered the president's office. I took off my jacket and hung it on the coat rack, then sat down at the desk which had several documents waiting on it. There was a draft of a study by a new editor, as well as a publicity document for an international book fair. At the very bottom were a cutout of a newly-published newspaper advertisement, a tentative outline for a second ad, and a table of advertising fees, all very clearly arranged.

It took me no longer than ten minutes to examine them. I answered the intercom and the editor in chief entered my office. Wearing a colorless blouse beneath her gray suit, she had the characteristic dry and passive expression of one who'd worked in an office for a long time.

"Has the office director left?"

"Yes."

"None of his family went to see him off, did they?"

"The agreements and procedures have all been carried out, so what does his family have to do with it?"

"With his training period at an end now, he won't ever be coming back, will he?"

"Ever?" I furrowed my brow. "He's only taking a bit of a break. He hasn't had any time off in over ten years, you know."

"It's been even longer for you, sir, and for the owner, it's worse."

"Is that so?"

"All the new employees met the department heads at the morning meeting. When they get back from lunch, I think they'd like to meet you, too, sir. Do you have time?"

I checked my schedule and saw that I had two conferences, a meeting outside the office, and even an appointment in the evening. It wasn't absolutely necessary for me to attend any of them. The company was no longer controlled by the individual ability and will of its executives, but ran in accordance with a stably-operating system. For the past ten years, I'd managed the company boldly, one could say almost aggressively. I'd entrusted J with all practical affairs, from reviewing manuscripts and deciding whether to publish them, to introducing writers to agencies. Publishers, under the cause of cultural enterprise, occasionally concentrated their efforts on receiving a tax exemption by openly speculating on land. After producing a bestseller, in many cases they no longer invested in publishing and instead focused their resources on more profitable side ventures. I even saw publishers who were only concerned with federal or municipal budgets, or getting into positions of authority to protect their interests. You could say that it was a means for small industries to survive. In such a current, it was my style to choose profit before justification. But I rarely ignored the advice of J, who clung almost obsessively to good books. While I increased the size of the company, J caused it to grow in quality.

When I first arrived, I was a lowly office worker in the

publishing department of a news organization. Three years later, I became editor in chief, and two years after that, when they tried to get rid of the book publishing department because it wasn't profitable, I took charge and turned it into the 30 billion won per year business it is today. The unstoppable proliferation of venture business at the time helped me to broaden our domain with overseas publishing agencies and culture programs, travel agencies, publishing consultation, and cultural investment financing. I even received recognition from a few cultural foundations and related government departments. Nicknames such as "Razor Blade" and "Siberia" have followed me ever since. These nicknames inevitably lacked imagination, like calling someone with curly hair "Ramen," or a stutterer "Motorbike," but there were in fact only so many nicknames one could give to a rational and realistic character like me. Even my friends addressed me by my title, not by my real name. Not friends from my youth, of course, like K and M, but the people I'd gotten close to through work.

I found the manuscript at the bottom of the pile of documents after the editor in chief had left. The examination of manuscripts was the jurisdiction of J and the editing committee, so it was rare to find a novel on my desk. In the corner of the cover page, "Needs further review" was written in J's hand. I casually glanced at the title. *The Cosmonauts in 1991.* The name of the author was unfamiliar to me. In any case, it was obviously a pen name. Cosmonaut was the word for a Russian astronaut, so it wasn't hard to guess that the significance of 1991 was the collapse of the Soviet Union.

At around twenty past one, the new employees came in to greet me. I felt the room grow stuffy, the air inside defiled. In addition to the sheer number of people that came in all at once, it was the disorganized energy and ambition emitting from each one's youthfulness that disturbed the room so much.

I don't envy young people. They hardly know anything, and they have neither money nor capable friends. They have fresh blood flowing into their brains and muscles, and with their ample supply of passion and time, countless possibilities are open to them. I arrived where I am today by going through that process. I think I'd rather fully enjoy what I have at this point than return to my youth and go through the difficult process of attaining it all again. People who get old with the inability to accept their age are full of self-pity, and cannot escape the gradual descent into loneliness that comes with it. Compared to them, I'm very realistic.

Before I go to work, I sometimes stare at myself in the mirror. The impression of my pillow on my cheek from the previous night's sleep stays there for hours. My drooping eyelids and the fine wrinkles around my mouth remind me of my father, who in my childhood would sit me down next to him so I could pull out his white hairs. But just as my increasing ability to maintain a certain balance in my bank account is the product of accruing age and time, so too is the loss of elasticity in my face. Since the onset of aging eyes, I've given up trying to read the small print on the menu when I go to an expensive restaurant; instead, I'll call the waiter over to recommend an appropriate meal for me, as if it were the more refined way. Even when I go to my favorite wine bar, I can no longer read the labels on the newly imported wine. Back when when my eyesight was still good, however, I couldn't even afford to hold a bottle of a high-quality wine, let alone look over its label. Isn't human life like that, maintaining a regular shape by moving around the irregular parts little by little? Childishness and poverty are the only things I remember from my youth.

After the new employees left, I opened the window and lit a cigarette. The manuscript I'd pushed to the corner of my desk, "The Cosmonauts in 1991," caught my eye again. I tried the intercom, but the editor in chief was not at her desk. I put out my cigarette, absent-mindedly pulled the manuscript toward me and began to read it, page after page.

I had been reading for about an hour when, at around two thirty, the message, "You've got mail," popped up on my computer screen, accompanied by a short alert sound. I closed the manuscript and opened my email box. The subject line was, "You've haven't forgotten about our appointment, have you?" I recalled once having trouble closing my browser window after I'd opened spam with a similar subject line. The sender's address was unfamiliar, too, but I clicked on the mail anyway. I'd been contemplating going out to get something to eat, so I was in no mood to linger. The email had only three lines. "We have an appointment today. I will be waiting for you at the River Seine at 8:00. Eun-sook." I deleted the mail and rose from my chair to see a haze of yellow dust rising outside. It was as if a reddish-gray filter was hanging down over the window. The cityscape looked unreal, like a grainy old documentary program. When I got out of the elevator and stepped outside the building, the wind blew into my face, as if it'd been waiting for me.

I was certain I'd read that manuscript before, but I couldn't remember where I'd seen it. If it was something I'd read when I was editor in chief, J would know and would have no reason to put a rejected manuscript on my desk. I thought about the time, right after I graduated from college, when I was so promptly rejected at every place I applied for work. I was working part-time as a proofreader at my college senior's publishing company, and I'd read a lot of the manuscripts circulating around the office in my abundant free time. But surely the contents of manuscripts I read well over ten years ago don't remain in my memory. Besides, I can hardly remember anything at all from that period of my life, as strange as it may sound. I only remember climbing up the creaking stairs of the wooden building to the sad-looking office, with a coal stove and a small blackboard hanging on the wall behind an iron desk. It was a time when I'd spend my bus fare on a bottle of soju and walk home instead, drinking and shouting into the night, "Nothing is impossible!" Even today, when people I don't know occasionally approach me as if they know me, I assume they're people I knew in those days. Needless to say, I'm not very happy to meet people from that most miserable period of my life.

"Humans have to some extent the ability to forget the things they don't want to remember, and for this reason they are flawed beings, not genuine at all." I think K was the first to tell me that. Ever serious and pedantic, K even wrote something similar on his suicide note. "Selective memory will allow you to soon forget all about me." True to his words, I hardly ever think about him. Nor M, who hasn't been back since he left for Germany fifteen years ago. But without those two, those days would've been meaningless and not worth remembering.

I felt like eating something spicy like pan-broiled octopus to bring back my appetite, but I opted for a pasta restaurant where I could sit alone comfortably. As mealtime had already passed, there were some vacant window tables. It wasn't long ago that I'd avoid tables by the window in brightly-lit restaurants because I felt like I was on display to the outside. But as I ate out alone more and more often, I noticed that it was surprisingly uncommon for passersby to look in on the inside of the restaurant. They were looking at their own reflections in the glass.

As I waited for my scampi in cream sauce, I tried to recall everyone I knew with the name Eun-sook. I lost interest after the sixth one. Thinking only of the business cards I'd received over the last twenty or so years, I realized Eun-sook was a very common name. Off the top of my head, I could even think of two Eun-sooks employed in my own company. The owner of a basement café I frequented until a few years ago was named Eun-sook, as was the realtor who introduced me to my current residence. Staying with my original impression of the email, I concluded that it was some kind of gag. But as I took a sip of the strongly acidic Colombian coffee the server had recommended, a new Eun-sook suddenly occurred to me. She had big eyes, a somewhat pale face, and she showed her pointed canines when she smiled. She was constantly surrounded by a dense, chain smoker's smoke, and her shoulder bag was always full of photocopies.

"Do you like music?" she asked me one day.

"I don't know. Why do you ask?" I gave her a bewildered look.

She smiled sweetly, pointing at my T-shirt with her finger. It was a faded mustard yellow T-shirt with musical notes printed randomly over it, something I wore only on days I overslept. In a poor family with lots of brothers, only the most dreadful clothes were left to the one who woke up last. Yes, I attended her wedding, too. How could I have completely forgotten about something like that? Three forty-five. There were only about four hours left until my alleged appointment with the woman. I had no reason to believe that it was that Eun-sook who sent the email. I slowly took another sip of coffee, savoring its aroma.

J might have been able to help if he were still around. I'd get drunk with him, play up my fatigue, show him the weak side of me that I wouldn't even show my wife. His memory was pretty good, too. I used to say that it was better to ask J about me than it was to ask me. He didn't have the need I had to forget about, say, something from my miserable years. But he's in an airplane now, at an altitude of over 10,000 meters.

"Brother." At the airport, J had called me by the name he used to call me when we were in university all those years ago. "Other things are nothing. This is hard."

"What are you talking about?" I looked casually at his face.

He was staring into empty space. "It's not like there wasn't another way. But I found that it was something I didn't want to do. I know that there's someone who can help me if I just open the door, but I don't feel like getting up. So I just sit there and get beaten."

"Beaten? By whom?"

J smiled bitterly, perhaps at the severity of my response. "I know why you talked me out of it. Like you said, leaving isn't going to make much of a difference, and I can't very well start something new right away. But you know me. I didn't want to end up just sitting around. Shouldn't I at least once live my life how I want? There's still enough time left for that, isn't there?"

When I came back to my office, the clock showed five after four. I sat down and opened my browser. I typed "River Seine" into the search engine, but none of the results were what I wanted. I typed "Café River Seine." Five results came up, but they had nothing to do with the place I was looking for. "River City" was a café on a boat, and there was information about various kinds of banquets and water sports. "River Thames" was there, but London, like Paris, was too far away. When I entered "Seine Café," there was one result, but it was for a place in Kangwon Province. Four hours was enough time to get there, but to go all that way was possible only if I knew for certain that it was the right place, and if I left right away. It also occurred to me that the Seine Café might not be an actual café, but an internet café.

K, M, and I had all gone to Eun-sook's wedding together. M's girlfriend, who stuck close to him day and night, had been there, too. When the ceremony was finished, we went to a movie. Then I seem to recall going to a bar when it got dark, as we normally did. We probably drank our fill of cheap alcohol without any food to go along with it and staggered back to our respective homes as usual. That day, as friends of the bride, we should've received envelopes filled with cash to have a small party at a café. The name of that café might have been River Seine. Surely Eun-sook must've been to the place before if she knew about it. Did she and I ever meet at a café, just the two of us? I don't recall any such place. But we'd agreed to meet there today, according to the email. Still, even if that much is true, I can't think of any reason at all why we'd need to see each other.

The editor in chief showed up thirty minutes later. She looked much neater with her suit jacket off, possibly because her blouse had short sleeves. Her skirt seemed shorter, too. She was holding a flower pot of royal azaleas that an employee of a client had brought. The vivid pink flowers, sticking their heads through the light green leaves, were splendid.

"What do you think? Don't they bring your office to life?" When she'd set the flower pot down, she rested one hand on the corner of my desk and leaned there with her entire body slanting. "Have you been looking for me?" When I put her in charge of my entire afternoon schedule, she raised her eyebrows. "About this contribution. Do you have the writer's contact information?"

"No."

"The director left without saying anything?" She saw the memo on my desk. "River Seine?"

"Do you by any chance know the place?"

She tilted her head as if in thought and then replied, "I think I've seen it somewhere – isn't it the name of a motel?" I felt she might have been right.

"So you really aren't going to the meetings with the administration department and the planning committee?" she continued.

"No."

"You seem unmotivated these days, sir."

"What, do you want to take over my position?"

"That's it exactly. You've been neglecting your duties, so please submit a written explanation. Either that, or take one week's vacation."

"It sounds like I'm becoming less and less needed at this company."

"Don't say that. Please just give that depression clinic I told you about a try. Shall I give you an initial diagnosis? You're always tired, and your body feels like it's dragging, right?"

"Yes."

"Your power of concentration is slipping, as is your memory?"

"It seems so."

"And you find it difficult to make decisions?"

"No, I don't, actually."

"Do you consider yourself a pessimist?"

"Very recently, I suppose."

"Then how about this. You've lost interest in things you used to enjoy, haven't you?"

"Well, like what, for example?"

Without giving a reply, the editor in chief smiled and left the room, her shoes click-clacking against the floor. "River Seine, I'll let you know if I remember where it is." Only then did I understand the significance of her last question.

I was about to light a cigarette with the disposable lighter J had left behind when a thought occurred to me. During a period when J came regularly to the morning meetings reeking of alcohol, he'd fish around in his pocket and pull out lighters, one after another, that he'd gotten from places he couldn't remember. The lighter in my hand, however, didn't say "River Seine," but "Friend Karaoke."

The Soviet Union vanished from the earth on December 24th, 1991. And 1992 was the year I started working in the news company's publishing department, the first job I had that could be called a regular job. Just out of college, J started working there at the same time. Our first day of work, to which we both wore suits, was in late spring. The first green flower buds were ready to burst, the sky was clear and free of yellow dust, and the city center was burgeoning with the activity of a new workday. The company was on the eighth floor of a marble building with an elevator. There was a computer on my desk, and through the large windows, Namsan Tower could be seen rising majestically.

Only a week earlier, I'd been hunched over an iron desk in a dimly-lit office in a two-story building buried deep down some side street, proofreading material with a red pen in hand. In those days, I'd always walk around with a black vinyl bag at my side, and if I went to a place where I had to remove my shoes, I kept my toes curled up and stole glances at my heels to make sure there weren't any holes in my socks. At drinking places, there was no such rule for shoe removal. Once, at a cheap *naengmyeon* restaurant bustling with a lunchtime crowd, someone actually took my old shoes and left a pair of new ones. A few days later, I went back to the restaurant in a joyful mood, actually knowing the comfort of wearing watertight shoes for the first time in years. The owner recognized me, and when he brought out my old shoes with obvious displeasure, I realized I'd done something wrong. I would've come to blows with him, who nearly took the shoes from my feet by force, if K hadn't put a stop to it. I'd wander aimlessly in those days, checking out used bookstores, and then, toward dawn, wake up in some strange place. Eun-sook's wedding day would have been one of those days.

Packed in among the throng of well-wishers, we jabbered incessantly while we ate *galbitang*. There were five of us, I believe, for there was an extra chair pulled up to a table seating four. K was there, as were M and his girlfriend. I can't remember who the fifth person was. K and M were both wearing limp, awkward-looking suits, and I'd been unable to change clothes and was wearing the same blue jacket with the hole in the pocket that I'd worn the previous day. Although the *galbitang* was getting cold, the air inside the reception restaurant was very hot. I couldn't take off my jacket because the red pen inside the chest pocket of the shirt with the musical notes on it had leaked ink into a large stain, so I was sweating like a pig. We carried on at the top of our voices, as if not doing so was not an option.

Our conversation was momentarily interrupted when the bride and groom entered the restaurant to greet their guests.

"Thank you for coming." Eun-sook extended a formal greeting to us in a flashy pink dress. Her large eyes were focused somewhere else.

"Where are you going on your honeymoon?" one of us asked, and the groom said something in reply, but I couldn't hear what he said from where I was sitting. I had a clear view of Eun-sook's profile, which kept disappearing and reappearing because the person sitting next to me in the extra chair we'd pulled up was turning his head from the bride to the groom. She was staring unwaveringly at some other place, not looking any one of us in the eyes. "Don't forget to invite us to your housewarming," M said cheerfully.

"Eun-sook, you look very pretty. I wonder when I'll get to wear a dress like that." M's girlfriend seemed truly envious.

K offered some similar words of encouragement. "Unlike the rest of us, you'll be happy even in April, the cruelest of months."

The person sitting next to me and I were the only ones who didn't say anything. As soon as the bride and groom moved on to another table, I got the chatter going again.

Just then, someone interrupted me. "Are you sad that Eun-sook got married?"

With that one remark, they all started in on me.

"You secretly liked her, didn't you?"

"No, I think you're under the illusion that she liked you."

"So now you feel like you've been betrayed, is that it?"

"I can't even imagine you with Eun-sook."

"Do you need to see her again?" K and M started to giggle, and M's girlfriend glared at M to stop.

"Let's go have drinks," I said. The person sitting next to me then politely suggested that we first go to the movie theater and stay until the sun sets because drinking in the daytime, especially in spring, was dangerous. I picked up my black vinyl bag from the restaurant floor and held it at my side. I think it was K who always told me to be careful not to lose my bag. I somehow ending up leading the way, and as I opened the door, with the sun shining down on my face, dazzling my eyes, I turned and glanced back at my friends. I clearly remember feeling somewhat sad as I took a step out into the bright street. It's strange. As a forgotten day from my youth came vividly back to life, everything in the present began to feel unreal.

3

Chapter 5: The Return of the Cosmonauts

With the Vostok launch close at hand, only the third of a total of six trials had been successful. The first spacecraft went off course and was lost in space, and others exploded or burned up. An accident exactly one year earlier in which a fueled rocket waiting for launch exploded, killing 268 people, caused the national news agency Itar-Tass to prepare the obituary of Yuri Gagarin, on board the Vostok, in advance. On the day of the launch, a few minutes before lift-off, a problem was discovered with the device keeping the doorway of the spacecraft airtight. One by one, the thirty-two bolts on the cover had to be loosened and then retightened. As soon as the spacecraft detached from the rocket, it went into a pirouette and nearly drifted off course. There was even a problem with the oxygen supply mechanism in the space suits. At the end of the flight when the spacecraft had returned to earth, the possibility of it landing safely on the ground was not high with Soviet technology of the time. Yuri Gagarin used the ejection seat to escape from the spacecraft at an altitude of 7,000 meters and came down to the ground by parachute. This was kept secret because the Fédération Aéronautique Internationale would acknowledge the feat only if the spacecraft was manned for both takeoff and landing. Yuri Gagarin was the first human to fly in outer space, which means that he was the first among those who left the earth for space to actually return.

M did not acknowledge Yuri Gagarin. He maintained that the Soviet cosmonauts who'd gone into space and disappeared forever were indeed the real heroes. The Soviets had sent up the first manned spacecraft in a technologically imperfect state in order to beat the Americans to it. Of course, they left no record of the incident. It would all have been made public had they succeeded, but they didn't, so the missing Cosmonauts were buried in darkness forever. "It's precisely the existence of these missing cosmonauts that exposes the violent duplicity of the socialist Soviets," M would rant.

A year before Gagarin's successful space flight, Italian radio operators had picked up human voices coming from space.

"S.O.S. to the whole world!"

"Hey, it's no use. Who'll come to save us when no one even knows we're here?"

It was in Russian. Soviet authorities disposed of the missing cosmonauts' personal documents, and even airbrushed their faces out of all group photographs. There was no sign of the cosmonauts' existence on earth, but their remains would drift in space for eternity.

K's concerns lay elsewhere. He gravely accepted the cosmonauts' state of panic upon returning after the collapse of the Soviet Union as his own. Colonel Yury Romanenko spent 326 days aboard the space station Mir. In a place where night and day remained unchanged and the sun rose and set twice every twenty-four hours, he ate only food from tubes and had to tie his body down when he slept. Romanenko's long exile opened up the possibility for humankind to colonize space. The Soviets had been deprived of being the first to land on the moon, but they regained supremacy over the Americans with the space station. The cosmonauts were heroes. Now, however, their glorious homeland was disappearing. After 1991, with Russia in chaos, the world would inevitably become a stranger and more frightening place to the cosmonauts than even space.

What had started as an argument over drinks that night gradually turned into a fight as they became more intoxicated. They spoke with rage, using language usually found on a propaganda poster.

"Let's drink to the garbage in space! Hey, build a monument to them and blast it out there! And why don't we hold a funeral for human barbarism while we're at it?"

"Give it a rest! Just think of the chaos then, when the cosmonauts came back from distant space to find that their homeland was gone. Whether they colonized the boundless cosmos or not, what changed their lives was the political reality of their country!"

"You sure love the homeland. If you want to suppress violence, all you need is a hero. What for, the liberation of the people? Should that cause such an immediate collapse?"

"You know it happened like that because the place is swarming with naïve anarchists like you, don't you?"

"Right. I have no intention, either, of wrangling with freaks like you over this bloody land. Can you live in a completely hopeless, backward country, struggling like an insect to survive? I'm leaving first thing tomorrow. I'll never set foot here again!"

"You treacherous bastard!"

"If I'm a traitor, then you're a dogmatist!"

"Do you want to have a go? Fine, let's do it! I'm ready to sacrifice myself as a warning shot to this damn world and its chaos of ideologies."

"You know, I'm so fed up with assholes like you and your poses that I've already turned my back."

"Shut your trap and put 'em up!"

"Okay, come on. You bastard!"

K picked up his glass and smashed it on the floor, and at almost the exact same time, M pushed the table back and stood up.

M's girlfriend, who hadn't left his side even for a moment

and would normally have been making a sharp criticism on the
obligation forced only upon women to maintain their virginity,
was wedging herself between K and M as the argument esca-
lated. With night deepening, she'd fallen asleep flat on the table
at some point, snoring now and then as if voicing a grievance
with M. What had awoken her was the sound of K and M
struggling to take hold of one another. She shot up and with a
lightning quick movement slapped M on the cheek, shouting,
"You prick!" With the three of them taking turns sitting and
standing around a table dizzyingly scattered with liquor bottles,
a quarrel was averted.

I too was drunk beyond my control then. I'd taken pens
one by one from my pockets, and I'd torn a page out of the
manuscript in my bag and scribbled something. Maybe I just
wanted to act drunk, even for myself, since I knew no one was
paying any attention to me. Actually, around that time in my life
I'd get teary-eyed at the slightest provocation, and then in that
mood scribble down something resembling poetry. I thought
that everything in the world had a special significance, so I
would always seek to learn what I could from anything, no
matter how trivial it may seem.

I suddenly came to my senses walking across a bridge over the
Han River with dried vomit on my sleeve and my pants wet in
the front. I didn't have my black vinyl bag. I stopped periodically
to lean my staggering body over the bridge railing and stare at
the light from the lampposts shimmering in the black water. I
felt my hot cheeks cool down.

I wonder if that was the day I wrote the letter to Eun-sook.
And if I actually sent it, and if it contained lines like, let's meet
on this day in exactly fifteen years. Would she have believed it
despite all the ambiguity and uncertainty? I wonder if there was
a time when we loved each other. It was a sincere letter, but it
was full of childish sentences. I think the last line was especially
touching, something like, "I'll remember you for the rest of my
life. You and I, the lonely Cosmonauts. Our point of return was

at River Seine. Farewell, my youth. Oh, Yuri Gagarin's blue star."

I wonder if I said the same thing when I tossed the bag carrying the manuscript down into the river. "Don't chase after some achievement as brilliant as the lights in the river. Don't ever hurry, even if your dreams turn like the orbit of the moon. Don't rush your stupid, poor ideas like an insect in the ground that doesn't open its eyes. Farewell, my youth. Oh, Yuri Gagarin's blue star."

At 6:35, the editor in chief called again on the intercom. "Sir, I just found out something by chance while speaking with my friend on the phone. She said there's a café near her office called River Seine." Before she could say anything else, I envisioned a dimly-lit room clouded with smoke. It was after I'd already remembered that the place was close to my senior's publishing company where I'd worked as a part-time proofreader. Lampshades with a red checked pattern and wooden tables covered with graffiti. A few *chansons* were repeated endlessly at regular intervals, and Eun-sook and I were the only patrons left at closing time. I always felt choked up when I was around her, and I don't think it was only because of the cigarette smoke.

With my vinyl bag at my side, I'm climbing the wooden stairs to the publishing company. K climbed those stairs, too, when he came looking for me carrying the manuscript of a novel written by one of his juniors. When I told him that I didn't know if a story about astronauts would work, K asked me to review the manuscript before he showed it to the boss. The junior may even have been J. Was J also the one sitting next to me at Eun-sook's wedding? I'm not sure. The one certainty is that J has eaten his in-flight meal by now and has probably fallen asleep with earphones in his ears. And because I lost that manuscript fifteen years ago, the author, whoever it was, wrote the whole thing again right from the beginning. Life goes by, so it can't be changed. But maybe a story that has passed can be rewritten.

The Cosmonauts in 1991

Chapter 6: Farewell, my Youth

Twenty-seven-year-old Soviet Lieutenant Yuri Gagarin left the earth at around nine o'clock in the morning. No one knew what would come of sending humankind into space. Inside the single-passenger spacecraft Vostok, meaning "east," Gagarin breathed in oxygen through his spacesuit. When he arrived in outer space, he swam like a fetus in a womb, and holding his breath like a baby ready to be born, he waved his arms. Floating all alone in the heart of a deep blackness tens of thousands of kilometers from Earth, Gagarin was already drifting away from the existence of his ego. With everything dark and weightless, it was like nothingness. He was anxious and lonely. Just then, a globe shining with light appeared before Yuri Gagarin's eyes. In the very middle of a universe filled with black empty space, a beautiful star was there, floating mysteriously. Gagarin trembled. "Is this why I penetrated space and travelled such a distance, just to see that star?" Finally, Yuri Gagarin muttered toward the star he had left and into which he would once again be born: "April 12th, 1961. The Earth is blue."

I left work at exactly seven o'clock. Finding a long-unused briefcase in the bottom drawer of my filing cabinet, I dusted it off and put the manuscript inside. I didn't meet anyone in the six-floor elevator trip down. The whole world was strangely quiet, like a still image. The only distinct sound was the sound of my footsteps.

The Earth's blueness signifies that it's a planet of water. Even J, looking down at Los Angeles from the sky, would be able to see the blue water of the swimming pools between the palm trees. Like Yuri Gagarin, J went on a long journey in order to see his own world from a distance. To renew himself thoroughly, he left his youth and his cigarettes with me.

Today I could be standing, just for a moment, at the cross-roads of time. In Yuri Gagarin's world, it may be possible to fold time as one does with origami. When I think of time as a long belt, a very long space lies between the day I went to that woman's wedding fifteen years ago and today. If I took the period of time from the wedding to yesterday, folded it up and sent it to a black hole, everything would be different. It would slip through the black hole and move to another dimension. Fifteen years of time, including the wedding, would vanish. Then she wouldn't have gotten married, and I wouldn't have thrown away the manuscript. K wouldn't be dead, and M wouldn't have yet left for Germany. My letter wouldn't yet be written. And because the day after that day would be today, I could go and meet Eun-sook carrying the briefcase containing the manuscript. The Blue Star that was thrown into the river would've been retrieved and put into a different briefcase.

Tomorrow morning I should hear from J that he's arrived. He's at an altitude of ten thousand meters now, and we're completely cut off. I also feel cut off from the world's time, as well as from all the days of my life. Tonight's an exception, an unknown time that doesn't belong anywhere in my life. It's gradually getting darker. The spring night envelops the streets in a mysterious light. Deep into the alleys, the air is filled with the scent of flowers, and the stars are cold and distinct.

Every time a poem flows from my mouth, my heart aches. With hot tears running from my eyes down to the ground, I lament the end of love. The air in the alley is damp from the breath of my drunken friends who've come outside to urinate. The high musical notes drawn dizzyingly on my t-shirt wobble endlessly up into the air. Beyond the sound of a glass breaking and a woman's muffled cries in some bar, someone's singing a song in a trembling voice. Someone's in the corner with a red pen, writing a letter without spaces, and his friends are crouching in the alley, sharing a cigarette, when, without realizing it, they all look up at the stars in the sky. Yuri Gagarin's beautiful and troubled youth is up there, too. From a spring night in 1992 at River Seine, the point of our return.

EUN HEEKYUNG made her entrance to the Korean literary scene in 1995 with her short novel Duet. The next year she won the Munhakdongne Fiction Award for her novel *A Gift from a Bird*, which portrayed the world of adults through the skeptical eyes of a 12-year-old narrator. Since her debut she has written ten books, including six collections of short stories and four novels. *Secrets and Lies*, published in 2005, is the three-generation story of two interrelated families.

YOONJIN PARK and CRAIG BOTT are married and live in Canada with their two daughters. This is their first published translation.

SORA KIM-RUSSELL is a Korean-American poet and translator originally from California and now living in Seoul, South Korea. Her translations include Gong Ji-young's *Our Happy Times* (Short Books, 2014) and Shin Kyung-sook's *I'll Be Right There* (Other Press, 2014). She teaches at Ewha Womans University.

JAE WON CHUNG was born in Seoul and lives in New York.

MICHAL AJVAZ, *The Golden Age.*
The Other City.
PIERRE ALBERT-BIROT, *Grabinoulor.*
YUZ ALESHKOVSKY, *Kangaroo.*
FELIPE ALFAU, *Chromos.*
Locos.
JOE AMATO, *Samuel Taylor's Last Night.*
IVAN ÂNGELO, *The Celebration.*
The Tower of Glass.
ANTÓNIO LOBO ANTUNES, *Knowledge of Hell.*
The Splendor of Portugal.
ALAIN ARIAS-MISSON, *Theatre of Incest.*
JOHN ASHBERY & JAMES SCHUYLER, *A Nest of Ninnies.*
ROBERT ASHLEY, *Perfect Lives.*
GABRIELA AVIGUR-ROTEM, *Heatwave and Crazy Birds.*
DJUNA BARNES, *Ladies Almanack.*
Ryder.
JOHN BARTH, *Letters.*
Sabbatical.
DONALD BARTHELME, *The King.*
Paradise.
SVETISLAV BASARA, *Chinese Letter.*
MIQUEL BAUÇÀ, *The Siege in the Room.*
RENÉ BELLETTO, *Dying.*
MAREK BIENCZYK, *Transparency.*
ANDREI BITOV, *Pushkin House.*
ANDREJ BLATNIK, *You Do Understand.*
Law of Desire.
LOUIS PAUL BOON, *Chapel Road.*
My Little War.
Summer in Termuren.
ROGER BOYLAN, *Killoyle.*
IGNÁCIO DE LOYOLA BRANDÃO, *Anonymous Celebrity.*
Zero.
BONNIE BREMSER, *Troia: Mexican Memoirs.*
CHRISTINE BROOKE-ROSE, *Amalgamemnon.*
BRIGID BROPHY, *In Transit.*
The Prancing Novelist.

GERALD L. BRUNS, *Modern Poetry and the Idea of Language.*
GABRIELLE BURTON, *Heartbreak Hotel.*
MICHEL BUTOR, *Degrees.*
Mobile.
G. CABRERA INFANTE, *Infante's Inferno.*
Three Trapped Tigers.
JULIETA CAMPOS, *The Fear of Losing Eurydice.*
ANNE CARSON, *Eros the Bittersweet.*
ORLY CASTEL-BLOOM, *Dolly City.*
LOUIS-FERDINAND CÉLINE, *North.*
Conversations with Professor Y.
London Bridge.
MARIE CHAIX, *The Laurels of Lake Constance.*
HUGO CHARTERIS, *The Tide Is Right.*
ERIC CHEVILLARD, *Demolishing Nisard.*
The Author and Me.
MARC CHOLODENKO, *Mordechai Schamz.*
JOSHUA COHEN, *Witz.*
EMILY HOLMES COLEMAN, *The Shutter of Snow.*
ERIC CHEVILLARD, *The Author and Me.*
ROBERT COOVER, *A Night at the Movies.*
STANLEY CRAWFORD, *Log of the S.S. The Mrs Unguentine.*
Some Instructions to My Wife.
RENÉ CREVEL, *Putting My Foot in It.*
RALPH CUSACK, *Cadenza.*
NICHOLAS DELBANCO, *Sherbrookes.*
The Count of Concord.
NIGEL DENNIS, *Cards of Identity.*
PETER DIMOCK, *A Short Rhetoric for Leaving the Family.*
ARIEL DORFMAN, *Konfidenz.*
COLEMAN DOWELL, *Island People.*
Too Much Flesh and Jabez.
ARKADII DRAGOMOSHCHENKO, *Dust.*
RIKKI DUCORNET, *Phosphor in Dreamland.*
The Complete Butcher's Tales.

RIKKI DUCORNET (cont.), *The Jade Cabinet.*
The Fountains of Neptune.
WILLIAM EASTLAKE, *The Bamboo Bed.*
Castle Keep.
Lyric of the Circle Heart.
JEAN ECHENOZ, *Chopin's Move.*
STANLEY ELKIN, *A Bad Man.*
Criers and Kibitzers, Kibitzers and Criers.
The Dick Gibson Show.
The Franchiser.
The Living End.
Mrs. Ted Bliss.
FRANÇOIS EMMANUEL, *Invitation to a Voyage.*
PAUL EMOND, *The Dance of a Sham.*
SALVADOR ESPRIU, *Ariadne in the Grotesque Labyrinth.*
LESLIE A. FIEDLER, *Love and Death in the American Novel.*
JUAN FILLOY, *Op Oloop.*
ANDY FITCH, *Pop Poetics.*
GUSTAVE FLAUBERT, *Bouvard and Pécuchet.*
KASS FLEISHER, *Talking out of School.*
JON FOSSE, *Aliss at the Fire.*
Melancholy.
FORD MADOX FORD, *The March of Literature.*
MAX FRISCH, *I'm Not Stiller.*
Man in the Holocene.
CARLOS FUENTES, *Christopher Unborn.*
Distant Relations.
Terra Nostra.
Where the Air Is Clear.
TAKEHIKO FUKUNAGA, *Flowers of Grass.*
WILLIAM GADDIS, JR., *The Recognitions.*
JANICE GALLOWAY, *Foreign Parts.*
The Trick Is to Keep Breathing.
WILLIAM H. GASS, *Life Sentences.*
The Tunnel.
The World Within the Word.
Willie Masters' Lonesome Wife.
GÉRARD GAVARRY, *Hoppla! 1 2 3.*

ETIENNE GILSON, *The Arts of the Beautiful.*
Forms and Substances in the Arts.
C. S. GISCOMBE, *Giscome Road.*
Here.
DOUGLAS GLOVER, *Bad News of the Heart.*
WITOLD GOMBROWICZ, *A Kind of Testament.*
PAULO EMÍLIO SALES GOMES, *P's Three Women.*
GEORGI GOSPODINOV, *Natural Novel.*
JUAN GOYTISOLO, *Count Julian.*
Juan the Landless.
Makbara.
Marks of Identity.
HENRY GREEN, *Blindness.*
Concluding.
Doting.
Nothing.
JACK GREEN, *Fire the Bastards!*
JIŘÍ GRUŠA, *The Questionnaire.*
MELA HARTWIG, *Am I a Redundant Human Being?*
JOHN HAWKES, *The Passion Artist.*
Whistlejacket.
ELIZABETH HEIGHWAY, ED., *Contemporary Georgian Fiction.*
AIDAN HIGGINS, *Balcony of Europe.*
Blind Man's Bluff.
Bornholm Night-Ferry.
Langrishe, Go Down.
Scenes from a Receding Past.
KEIZO HINO, *Isle of Dreams.*
KAZUSHI HOSAKA, *Plainsong.*
ALDOUS HUXLEY, *Antic Hay.*
Point Counter Point.
Those Barren Leaves.
Time Must Have a Stop.
NAOYUKI II, *The Shadow of a Blue Cat.*
DRAGO JANČAR, *The Tree with No Name.*
MIKHEIL JAVAKHISHVILI, *Kvachi.*
GERT JONKE, *The Distant Sound.*
Homage to Czerny.
The System of Vienna.

FOR A FULL LIST OF PUBLICATIONS, VISIT: www.dalkeyarchive.com

JACQUES JOUET, *Mountain R.*

Savage.

Upstaged.

MIEKO KANAI, *The Word Book.*

YORAM KANIUK, *Life on Sandpaper.*

ZURAB KARUMIDZE, *Dagny.*

JOHN KELLY, *From Out of the City.*

HUGH KENNER, *Flaubert, Joyce and Beckett: The Stoic Comedians.*

Joyce's Voices.

DANILO KIŠ, *The Attic.*

The Lute and the Scars.

Psalm 44.

A Tomb for Boris Davidovich.

ANITA KONKKA, *A Fool's Paradise.*

GEORGE KONRÁD, *The City Builder.*

TADEUSZ KONWICKI, *A Minor Apocalypse.*

The Polish Complex.

ANNA KORDZAIA-SAMADASHVILI, *Me, Margarita.*

MENIS KOUMANDAREAS, *Koula.*

ELAINE KRAF, *The Princess of 72nd Street.*

JIM KRUSOE, *Iceland.*

AYSE KULIN, *Farewell: A Mansion in Occupied Istanbul.*

EMILIO LASCANO TEGUI, *On Elegance While Sleeping.*

ERIC LAURRENT, *Do Not Touch.*

VIOLETTE LEDUC, *La Bâtarde.*

EDOUARD LEVÉ, *Autoportrait.*

Newspaper.

Suicide.

Works.

MARIO LEVI, *Istanbul Was a Fairy Tale.*

DEBORAH LEVY, *Billy and Girl.*

JOSÉ LEZAMA LIMA, *Paradiso.*

ROSA LIKSOM, *Dark Paradise.*

OSMAN LINS, *Avalovara.*

The Queen of the Prisons of Greece.

FLORIAN LIPUŠ, *The Errors of Young Tjaž.*

GORDON LISH, *Peru.*

ALF MACLOCHLAINN, *Out of Focus.*

Past Habitual.

The Corpus in the Library.

RON LOEWINSOHN, *Magnetic Field(s).*

YURI LOTMAN, *Non-Memoirs.*

D. KEITH MANO, *Take Five.*

MINA LOY, *Stories and Essays of Mina Loy.*

MICHELINE AHARONIAN MARCOM, *A Brief History of Yes.*

The Mirror in the Well.

BEN MARCUS, *The Age of Wire and String.*

WALLACE MARKFIELD, *Teitlebaum's Window.*

DAVID MARKSON, *Reader's Block.*

Wittgenstein's Mistress.

CAROLE MASO, *AVA.*

HISAKI MATSUURA, *Triangle.*

LADISLAV MATEJKA & KRYSTYNA POMORSKA, EDS., *Readings in Russian Poetics: Formalist & Structuralist Views.*

HARRY MATHEWS, *Cigarettes.*

The Conversions.

The Human Country.

The Journalist.

My Life in CIA.

Singular Pleasures.

The Sinking of the Odradek.

Stadium.

Tlooth.

HISAKI MATSUURA, *Triangle.*

DONAL MCLAUGHLIN, *beheading the virgin mary, and other stories.*

JOSEPH MCELROY, *Night Soul and Other Stories.*

ABDELWAHAB MEDDEB, *Talismano.*

GERHARD MEIER, *Isle of the Dead.*

HERMAN MELVILLE, *The Confidence-Man.*

AMANDA MICHALOPOULOU, *I'd Like.*

STEVEN MILLHAUSER, *The Barnum Museum.*

In the Penny Arcade.

RALPH J. MILLS, JR., *Essays on Poetry.*

MOMUS, *The Book of Jokes.*

CHRISTINE MONTALBETTI, *The Origin of Man.*

Western.

NICHOLAS MOSLEY, *Accident.*
Assassins.
Catastrophe Practice.
A Garden of Trees.
Hopeful Monsters.
Imago Bird.
Inventing God.
Look at the Dark.
Metamorphosis.
Natalie Natalia.
Serpent.
WARREN MOTTE, *Fables of the Novel:*
French Fiction since 1990.
Fiction Now: The French Novel in the
21st Century.
Mirror Gazing.
Oulipo: A Primer of Potential Literature.
GERALD MURNANE, *Barley Patch.*
Inland.
YVES NAVARRE, *Our Share of Time.*
Sweet Tooth.
DOROTHY NELSON, *In Night's City.*
Tar and Feathers.
ESHKOL NEVO, *Homesick.*
WILFRIDO D. NOLLEDO, *But for*
the Lovers.
BORIS A. NOVAK, *The Master of*
Insomnia.
FLANN O'BRIEN, *At Swim-Two-Birds.*
The Best of Myles.
The Dalkey Archive.
The Hard Life.
The Poor Mouth.
The Third Policeman.
CLAUDE OLLIER, *The Mise-en-Scène.*
Wert and the Life Without End.
PATRIK OUŘEDNÍK, *Europeana.*
The Opportune Moment, 1855.
BORIS PAHOR, *Necropolis.*
FERNANDO DEL PASO, *News from*
the Empire.
Palinuro of Mexico.
ROBERT PINGET, *The Inquisitory.*
Mahu or The Material.
Trio.
MANUEL PUIG, *Betrayed by Rita*
Hayworth.

The Buenos Aires Affair.
Heartbreak Tango.
RAYMOND QUENEAU, *The Last Days.*
Odile.
Pierrot Mon Ami.
Saint Glinglin.
ANN QUIN, *Berg.*
Passages.
Three.
Tripticks.
ISHMAEL REED, *The Free-Lance*
Pallbearers.
The Last Days of Louisiana Red.
Ishmael Reed: The Plays.
Juice!
The Terrible Threes.
The Terrible Twos.
Yellow Back Radio Broke-Down.
JASIA REICHARDT, *15 Journeys Warsaw*
to London.
JOÃO UBALDO RIBEIRO, *House of the*
Fortunate Buddhas.
JEAN RICARDOU, *Place Names.*
RAINER MARIA RILKE,
The Notebooks of Malte Laurids Brigge.
JULIÁN RÍOS, *The House of Ulysses.*
Larva: A Midsummer Night's Babel.
Poundemonium.
ALAIN ROBBE-GRILLET, *Project for a*
Revolution in New York.
A Sentimental Novel.
AUGUSTO ROA BASTOS, *I the Supreme.*
DANIËL ROBBERECHTS, *Arriving in*
Avignon.
JEAN ROLIN, *The Explosion of the*
Radiator Hose.
OLIVIER ROLIN, *Hotel Crystal.*
ALIX CLEO ROUBAUD, *Alix's Journal.*
JACQUES ROUBAUD, *The Form of*
a City Changes Faster, Alas, Than the
Human Heart.
The Great Fire of London.
Hortense in Exile.
Hortense Is Abducted.
Mathematics: The Plurality of Worlds of
Lewis.
Some Thing Black.

RAYMOND ROUSSEL, *Impressions of Africa.*

VEDRANA RUDAN, *Night.*

PABLO M. RUIZ, *Four Cold Chapters on the Possibility of Literature.*

GERMAN SADULAEV, *The Maya Pill.*

TOMAŽ ŠALAMUN, *Soy Realidad.*

LYDIE SALVAYRE, *The Company of Ghosts. The Lecture. The Power of Flies.*

LUIS RAFAEL SÁNCHEZ, *Macho Camacho's Beat.*

SEVERO SARDUY, *Cobra & Maitreya.*

NATHALIE SARRAUTE, *Do You Hear Them? Martereau. The Planetarium.*

STIG SÆTERBAKKEN, *Siamese. Self-Control. Through the Night.*

ARNO SCHMIDT, *Collected Novellas. Collected Stories. Nobodaddy's Children. Two Novels.*

ASAF SCHURR, *Motti.*

GAIL SCOTT, *My Paris.*

DAMION SEARLS, *What We Were Doing and Where We Were Going.*

JUNE AKERS SEESE, *Is This What Other Women Feel Too?*

BERNARD SHARE, *Inish. Transit.*

VIKTOR SHKLOVSKY, *Bowstring. Literature and Cinematography. Theory of Prose. Third Factory. Zoo, or Letters Not about Love.*

PIERRE SINIAC, *The Collaborators.*

KJERSTI A. SKOMSVOLD, *The Faster I Walk, the Smaller I Am.*

JOSEF ŠKVORECKÝ, *The Engineer of Human Souls.*

GILBERT SORRENTINO, *Aberration of Starlight. Blue Pastoral. Crystal Vision.*

Imaginative Qualities of Actual Things. Mulligan Stew. Red the Fiend. Steelwork. Under the Shadow.

MARKO SOSIČ, *Ballerina, Ballerina.*

ANDRZEJ STASIUK, *Dukla. Fado.*

GERTRUDE STEIN, *The Making of Americans. A Novel of Thank You.*

LARS SVENDSEN, *A Philosophy of Evil.*

PIOTR SZEWC, *Annihilation.*

GONÇALO M. TAVARES, *A Man: Klaus Klump. Jerusalem. Learning to Pray in the Age of Technique.*

LUCIAN DAN TEODOROVICI, *Our Circus Presents...*

NIKANOR TERATOLOGEN, *Assisted Living.*

STEFAN THEMERSON, *Hobson's Island. The Mystery of the Sardine. Tom Harris.*

TAEKO TOMIOKA, *Building Waves.*

JOHN TOOMEY, *Sleepwalker.*

DUMITRU TSEPENEAG, *Hotel Europa. The Necessary Marriage. Pigeon Post. Vain Art of the Fugue.*

ESTHER TUSQUETS, *Stranded.*

DUBRAVKA UGRESIC, *Lend Me Your Character. Thank You for Not Reading.*

TOR ULVEN, *Replacement.*

MATI UNT, *Brecht at Night. Diary of a Blood Donor. Things in the Night.*

ÁLVARO URIBE & OLIVIA SEARS, EDS., *Best of Contemporary Mexican Fiction.*

ELOY URROZ, *Friction. The Obstacles.*

LUISA VALENZUELA, *Dark Desires and the Others. He Who Searches.*

PAUL VERHAEGHEN, *Omega Minor.*

BORIS VIAN, *Heartsnatcher.*

LLORENÇ VILLALONGA, *The Dolls' Room.*

TOOMAS VINT, *An Unending Landscape.*

ORNELA VORPSI, *The Country Where No One Ever Dies.*

AUSTRYN WAINHOUSE, *Hedyphagetica.*

CURTIS WHITE, *America's Magic Mountain.*
The Idea of Home.
Memories of My Father Watching TV.
Requiem.

DIANE WILLIAMS, *Excitability: Selected Stories.*
Romancer Erector.

DOUGLAS WOOLF, *Wall to Wall.*
Ya! & John-Juan.

JAY WRIGHT, *Polynomials and Pollen.*
The Presentable Art of Reading Absence.

PHILIP WYLIE, *Generation of Vipers.*

MARGUERITE YOUNG, *Angel in the Forest.*
Miss MacIntosh, My Darling.

REYOUNG, *Unbabbling.*

VLADO ŽABOT, *The Succubus.*

ZORAN ŽIVKOVIĆ , *Hidden Camera.*

LOUIS ZUKOFSKY, *Collected Fiction.*

VITOMIL ZUPAN, *Minuet for Guitar.*

SCOTT ZWIREN, *God Head.*

AND MORE . . .